All she had to say was no....

Instead, Julie unlocked the door of her apartment and held it open wide. Glorying in the heat from Angel's dark, passionate gaze, she couldn't dredge up a single reason to refuse him. As he followed her inside, she reached for the light switch, but his hand clamped her wrist.

"We have the moonlight," he said. Angel's electric blue eyes appeared black, and his face was somber. "Are you sure this is what you want?" he asked, his voice deep and heavy with desire.

Mingled fear and longing choked her. Later she would have the time to rebuild those walls around herself, she decided. To sort out the blame that stood between them. Tonight belonged to two high-school sweethearts who had never had a chance. Just this once, she meant to take what Angel was offering.

"I'm sure," she finally whispered. Just this once, she wanted to feel like the woman he had turned her into ten long years ago....

Dear Reader,

With her latest novel (of more than fifty!) on the stands this month, award-winning **Nora Roberts** shares her thoughts about Silhouette **Special Edition**:

"I still remember very clearly the feeling I experienced when I sold my first Silhouette **Special Edition**: absolute delight! The **Special Edition** line gave many writers like me an opportunity to grow with the romance genre. These books are indeed special because they allow us to create characters much like ourselves, people we can understand and root for. They are stories of love and hope and commitment. To me, that *is* romance."

Characters you can understand and root for, women and men who share your values, dream your dreams and tap deep inner sources of love and hope—they're a Silhouette **Special Edition** mainstay for six soul-satisfying romances each month. But do other elements—glamorous, faraway settings, intricate, flamboyant plots—sway your reading selections? This month's Silhouette **Special Edition** authors—Nora Roberts, Tracy Sinclair, Kate Meriwether, Pat Warren, Pamela Toth and Laurey Bright—will take you from Arizona to Australia and to points in between, sharing adventures (and misadventures!) of the heart along the way. We hope you'll savor all six novels.

Be like Nora Roberts—share your thoughts about Silhouette **Special Edition**. We welcome your comments.

Warmest wishes,

Leslie Kazanjian, Senior Editor
Silhouette Books
300 East 42nd Street
New York, N.Y. 10017

PAMELA TOTH
Dark Angel

Silhouette Special Edition

Published by Silhouette Books New York

America's Publisher of Contemporary Romance

This book is dedicated,
with respect and appreciation,
to Maureen Walters.

SILHOUETTE BOOKS
300 East 42nd St., New York, N.Y. 10017

ISBN: 0-373-09515-5

First Silhouette Books printing March 1989

All the characters in this book are fictitious. Any
resemblance to actual persons, living or dead, is
purely coincidental.

®: Trademark used under license and
registered in the United States Patent and
Trademark Office and in other countries.

Printed in the U.S.A.

PAMELA TOTH

was born in Wisconsin but now makes her home near Seattle, Washington, with her husband and two daughters. She enjoys bowling, roller-skating, and camping with her family, but for the last four years she has devoted much time to writing romances. Pamela says she gets many of her ideas simply from reading the newspaper, when various occupations and stories trigger her imagination to create original scenes and characters.

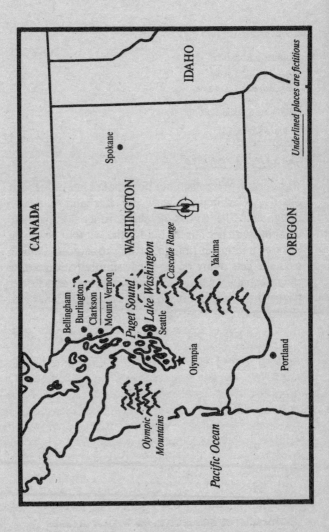

CANADA

WASHINGTON

IDAHO

Spokane

Bellingham
Burlington
Clarkson
Mount Vernon

Puget Sound
Lake Washington

Cascade Range

Seattle

Yakima

Olympia

Olympic
Mountains

OREGON

Portland

Pacific Ocean

Underlined places are fictitious

Chapter One

Angel Maneros whipped his black Ferrari onto the shoulder of the road and killed the engine. He uncurled his length from behind the wheel and walked to the edge of the wide space, his gaze behind the dark glasses sweeping across the Skagit Valley spread below. The greens and golds of its pastures and fields reminded him of an old patchwork quilt he'd had as a child. In the valley's center lay the town of Mount Vernon, and beyond it to the northwest his ultimate destination, Clarkson. Angel wanted to cup his hands to his face and shout that he was back for good. Instead he returned to the car, fired up its powerful engine and roared down the last hill of his long drive from California to western Washington.

He remembered when he'd left so long ago, full of pain and bitterness. Now he was returning, more successful than he had been in his wildest dreams.

A humorless smile twisted Angel's lips. How ironic that one of the town's most despised citizens would return as a celebrity, the local boy who'd made good. He would be fussed over and talked about as if he'd miraculously changed from the half-breed bastard they'd all looked down on to some kind of folk hero.

He thought of the few who mattered, his mother who was long since dead, his friend Joey who waited at the new house, his brother Luis. And Julie. His knuckles turned white against the leather-covered steering wheel, and he remembered her betrayal.

It had been somewhere between twilight and full dark that fall so many years before when Angel sauntered toward the back parking lot of the public library in Clarkson. His arm hung loosely across Ava Ruiz's shoulders, and his nostrils were full of her potent perfume as they strolled along, hips bumping, drawn by the sound of taunting voices. Angel and Ava hadn't been at the library to study; the big bushes along the building's side provided a measure of privacy for couples who had nowhere else to go.

Angel was keyed up and tense. Once again Ava had teased him until he was wild with need, then laughingly put him off. His teenage hormones were red-hot needles that stabbed at him insistently as he walked, but he was unwilling to let Ava see how she'd managed to tie him into knots again. She ran a hand across his waist, beneath his leather jacket, then shook back her long black hair as she tried to discover the extent of her victory.

"I didn't say we had to leave," she murmured, peering up at him with her big brown eyes. "You give up too easily."

Angel's expression was haughty as he glanced at her. "I was getting bored," he said, taking a little satisfaction at the way her full mouth twisted into a pout.

If Ava didn't quit playing games with him soon, he'd find another girlfriend. Ava was no virgin; few of the girls in his crowd still were. They were too hungry for affection. Their lives stretched before them with a predictability that gave little reason to deny what brief pleasures they could find along the way.

Angel moved his free arm, flexing the muscles that rippled beneath the deeply tanned skin. He might not have much, or be much, but he was just discovering that what he did have was enough to turn feminine heads away from the rich white boys who cruised the high school in cars their daddies had paid for. Right now that was almost enough.

When they rounded the corner, Angel saw the reason for the jeering laughter he'd heard moments before. Five of his buddies had cornered a girl in the back of the parking lot.

Dropping his arm from Ava's shoulders, Angel walked toward the group. It looked like some Anglo had used bad judgment in leaving the safety of the library alone.

Several heads turned as Angel stepped into the dim glow coming from an overhead light. The boys stood in the shadows beyond, forming a loose circle that effectively separated the girl from her red sports car.

Angel recognized the new Mustang he'd seen in the high school lot. One of the boys lounged against its side, facing Angel. He looked up with a cocky grin.

"*Amigo!* Look what we got. A hill chick."

The hilly area surrounding the golf course, past the outskirts of town, was where most of the rich families lived.

Angel narrowed his eyes and studied the girl, who was holding an armload of books protectively against her thin body. Her light brown hair fell to her shoulders, the ends turning under, and her eyes were wide with fear behind her glasses. Angel searched his mind to come up with a name. Judy Remington, something like that. She'd been in the algebra class he'd repeated the year before. Except for that, he couldn't remember ever noticing her around the school. She was a brain, but had been extremely shy and quiet in class—not the kind of girl a guy would remember. She wasn't a part of the rich crowd he despised, but he knew from her last name that she came from money. Her old man owned Olympic Frozen Foods, the town's largest employer of seasonal workers.

"Please let me go now," she said in a high voice as he stepped closer.

"What are you guys up to?"

One of the boys pulled out a switchblade, waving it slowly. He laughed as the girl gasped and shrank back.

At the look of pure terror on her face, Angel almost felt sorry for her, even if she was rich.

"We're just havin' a little fun," a boy named Rafe said. He was older and had a reputation for being as mean as a starved dog. Angel didn't like him.

"Yeah," the one with the knife echoed. "We're just havin' a little fun with 'miss white bread' here."

Angel hadn't planned to interfere, but the odds bothered him. He moved until he was in front of the boys and tossed back his straight hair. "No challenge to get a girl who's already scared of her own shadow," he said smoothly, looking into each face in turn. "She knows we're bad. Let's send her home."

He waited to see what they would do, his pose deceptively relaxed. Angel had no idea why he was bothering, except that the girl was frightened and outnumbered.

There was a moment of tense silence.

"Why don't you go back to your girlfriend," Rafe said, stepping forward. "And leave us to ours."

Someone giggled. Angel stood his ground, staring hard at the older boy, whose eyes were full of anger. Rafe wouldn't take Angel on in a fair fight, it wasn't his style. After a long moment, Rafe stepped back.

"She's too skinny anyhow," he sneered. "And too green for me." His attention flicked knowingly toward Ava. Angel caught his meaning; she'd been Rafe's girl the year before.

A couple of the boys shrugged and began to turn away. The fat one who'd been blocking the girl's car door looked at Angel with a worried expression.

"We weren't really going to hurt her," he whined.

"That's not what you said." The girl's voice was louder, accusing. When Angel looked back at her, she ducked her head, straight hair falling forward to shield her face.

"Come on, Joey," Rafe said. "This is boring. Let's go down to the bowling alley." He didn't look at Angel again.

"Angel, why you sticking up for *her*?"

He'd forgotten all about Ava, but now she was pulling at the edge of his black leather jacket. "Angel," she said again.

He ignored her. Served her right after what she'd done. Instead he walked over to where Joey still stood by the Remington girl's car.

"Do me a favor," he asked the fat boy, who perked up instantly. "Walk Ava home."

Her protests were drowned out by Joey's eager agreement. If Angel wanted something, Joey would be the first to do it for him, in this case whether Ava wanted to go or not.

She began to call Angel names as Joey gripped her arm and hauled her off. Angel continued to ignore her, watching the other girl instead.

Her attention veered from Joey to Angel as if she were trying to decide if he was a new threat. She was clearly too frozen with fear to move toward the now unblocked door of her car. Angel leaned forward slowly, took the keys from her unresisting fingers and opened the door.

"Judy, you okay?"

She took a deep breath. "Julianna," she said. "My name's Julianna."

She was pale in the lamplight. Angel hoped she wasn't going to do anything stupid like pass out.

"I'm okay," she said, her voice strained and high. "Thank you very much."

He wanted to laugh at her polite tone. Despite her fear, the words sounded as if the two of them had been drinking tea.

"You want a can of pop?" His offer surprised him almost as much as it obviously did her. Julianna's eyes widened behind the lenses of her glasses, darting from his long black hair to the bandanna tied around his head. She moistened her lips.

"There's a machine by the door," he said, feeling awkward. "You look like you could stand a shot of caffeine." Maybe she was afraid someone would see them together. Flushing, he was about to withdraw his offer when she spoke.

"Yes, I would. That's very nice of you." She smiled and he stared. Her whole face had changed subtly, and he suddenly realized that she was very pretty, despite her glasses and unattractive clothes.

He gestured toward the machine, digging in the pocket of his worn jeans for change. "I'll be right back."

He glanced over his shoulder before entering the building foyer. Perhaps she'd been waiting for him to turn away so she could jump in her car and leave. No, she still stood clutching her books. An unidentifiable feeling washed over Angel as he got two colas from the machine and walked back to the parking area. Rescuing chicks wasn't a normal pastime for him, but it made him feel kind of good. Usually girls like her would stare at him when they thought he wasn't looking, but they didn't speak, and they rarely smiled unless they were trying to tease him with what he couldn't have.

A middle-aged couple came out the door and headed toward their car. Angel tensed, half-fearful that Julianna might say something, pretending he'd been bothering her rather than let anyone think she was talking to him voluntarily. It was a small town and people gossiped.

She opened the car door and he thought she was leaving. A sickening wave of shame rose inside him, for a moment his cheeks burned. But she only tossed her books onto the seat.

Angel stopped, holding out one can of pop and making her step forward to take it. When her fingers curled around the can, their warmth surprised him. He had thought they'd be cold in the aftermath of what had happened, but she seemed to be loosening up. Perhaps it was only an act, though, part of the fancy training in politeness she'd had as one of the hill people. She tugged at the can, but he didn't release it. Her gaze flew to his.

"Let me open it for you," he said, pulling the can back. Again she ducked her head, and he noticed how shiny her hair was, like satin. He wanted to reach out and touch it, but he knew she'd run a mile if he did. Instead he opened both cans.

"Thank you," she said again, then laughed softly. "I keep saying that."

He took a long swallow of the soda, tilting his head back. When he looked down at her, she was sipping hers. She glanced at the tiny gold watch on her wrist. "I'd better go. My parents will be worried."

"Yeah." He knew a brush-off when he heard one.

"Thank you again," she said in the lengthening silence before turning back toward her car.

"Maybe I want more of a thank-you."

She almost dropped the pop can in her haste to open the door and slide into her little Mustang. Behind her, Angel laughed. He'd only meant it as a joke.

She shut the door and cautiously rolled the window down, never taking her gaze from him. Angel squatted down beside the car so they were at eye level.

"You move quick when you want," he said, still grinning.

After a moment Julianna grinned back as if she realized he'd been teasing her. To his surprise she stuck out her hand. He stared hard before realizing she meant for him to shake it. The contrast between their skin tones wasn't lost on him as he gripped her fingers briefly.

"I appreciate what you did," she murmured. "Now I have to get home." She started the engine.

Angel stood up. "Yeah, see you around."

She started to say something else, probably another thank-you, then just smiled instead and drove off. Angel watched her car's taillights until she turned onto the street. He was thinking that their paths wouldn't cross again. Except for a quirk of fate, they wouldn't have crossed this time. For some reason the thought depressed him. She'd been scared, but not scared of him, and she hadn't treated him the way so many of the townspeople did, as if there was a bad smell that hovered around him. She had been polite.

Angel was pleased with himself until he realized that a girl like Julianna had probably been taught to be polite to everyone, even a nobody like Angel Maneros. He crumpled his empty can with one hand and flung it far into the bushes beside the building before ramming his fists into the pockets of his worn jacket. His broad shoulders slumped forward as he turned and walked to the street. He was in no hurry to go home; his mother was working at the bar, and the small, hot apartment would be empty and silent except for the sounds of the neighbors' televisions and arguments.

Why, after all these silent years, was Angel Maneros returning to Clarkson?

Julie Remington flopped across the bed, staring up at the ruffled canopy she'd picked out as a teenager. The room was the same as it had been before she had left her parents' house, and now she was back. She studied the clock radio upside down until she figured out that it was still two hours until dinner. Not that she was hungry; since the divorce her appetite had dwindled.

Sitting up, she ran a hand through her tangled hair. It had grown long, and she usually wore it off her face. For the first few weeks after she had walked out on Brad, she'd given little thought to her appearance or plans for the future, but finally she'd gotten tired of inactivity and brooding and had begun a determined effort to get on with her life. Now, months later, she found herself looking forward to each new day and the challenges it would bring. When she did catch herself slipping backward, she remembered that other people had gone through worse. They became stronger for it, and she would, too.

Getting her hair trimmed was a small thing, but pride demanded she make the most of her appearance before she ran into the man who'd taken her love and tossed it away for reasons she had never understood. Clarkson was a small town, and they would meet eventually.

Julie thought about making an appointment at the beauty salon, then remembered that she hoped to be working the next day. She'd stop by the shop after school if she was called for a substitute teaching job. The hairdresser always fit her in, one benefit of having the family name she did—the name she'd taken back after her divorce from Bradley Hammond.

As always, the mere thought of Bradley sent icy chills across her skin. Before she was able to prevent it, his handsome blond image forced its way to the front of her mind. Julie was almost glad when another face, dark and dangerous, blotted out Brad's sneering expression.

Then the pain came, almost as strong as it had been ten years before when she realized that Angel had left town without her. A sudden flood of raw tears seeped between her lashes and trickled down her cheeks as she remembered the last time they had been together. Angel's voice had been soft with love, his eyes warm and caring as they had made their plans. She'd believed then that their love could survive any test, any threat.

Julie sat up and hurled her hairbrush at the wall. What a baby she'd been, seeing things in their high school romance that weren't really there. Angel had walked away without a qualm, leaving her behind like a rusted-out car.

She turned and buried her face in her pillow, desperately willing herself to only remember the hurt. Instead memories of kindness and unexpected compassion flooded into the cracks in her partially healed heart, breaking it once again.

The news of Angel's upcoming return had ripped open the door she usually kept firmly shut against the memories of that year they had become friends and then something more. A sob of despair and remembrance left her lips before she could prevent it.

The day after Angel rescued her from the group of hoods in the library parking lot, Julie found herself looking for him between every class. She didn't see him, even at lunch. Perhaps he'd skipped. Most of his friends did, if they hadn't dropped out already. Angel was a senior; Julie wondered why he was still in school.

It was at the end of the day, and she was on her way to the student parking lot when she finally saw him lounging against the side of the building, a cigarette dangling from his hand. Smoking at school was strictly forbidden, but from what she'd heard about him, Angel wasn't bothered by too many of the rules. He got mostly decent grades, but he was always in trouble, mouthing off at teachers, cutting class, hanging out in the halls with guys who were no longer students. The grapevine was always carrying stories about Angel's latest infractions.

Her steps slowed as she stared at his black boots, worn jeans and white T-shirt. When she got to his face she was mortified to see that he was staring back, a lazy grin curling his full mouth. His eyes were narrowed in the sunlight so that their brilliant blue was hidden. With the straight black hair brushing against his neck, and the dark skin taut across his handsome, narrow face, he looked inapproachable.

Julie hesitated, blushing. She had decided earlier that she really needed to thank him again, but now she wasn't so sure. He was alone, but that didn't mean the other kids wouldn't notice if she went over to talk to him. What Julie, the brainy misfit, did was hardly school news, but Angel's actions were always of great interest. What if he turned away when she approached, leaving her standing there alone? Just because he'd been nice the night before didn't mean he would be now. He had a reputation, and niceness wasn't part of it.

Julie's good breeding, and the manners that had been drilled into her since the cradle, took over. Her feet were moving in his direction before her brain made a conscious decision.

As she stopped in front of him, Angel took a last drag from the cigarette in his hand and crushed it beneath his boot. Smoke streamed from his thin nostrils, adding to the aura of toughness that surrounded him like a gang jacket.

"Hello," she said quietly, as he gazed down at her from beneath lowered lids, head tilted back and one black brow quirked.

"Hi." His voice was like the scrape of a cat's tongue, rough and smooth blended together.

Out of the corner of her eye, Julie saw Heather Bates and Ginger Cunningham pause to stare, whispering behind their hands. She thrust her chin out. Let them talk.

"I wanted to thank you again," she said quickly to get it over with.

"For what?" he drawled, obviously amused at her discomfort.

"Hi, Angel," Ginger called as she walked by. Julie glanced up to see the older girl bat her eyelashes and give him a big smile.

"Hiya, babe." Angel leered back before returning his attention to Julie.

"You know," she said, shifting her books from one arm to the other and barely resisting the urge to wet her dry lips. "For last night."

"Oh, that. No problem." Again he looked past her, as if her presence bored him.

Julie swallowed. "Well, uh, goodbye," she said, feeling absolutely stupid.

Angel straightened away from the wall, making her scamper backward. "You got your car here?" he asked.

She blinked in confusion. "Yes, I do." Her father had given her the red Mustang for her birthday to boost her popularity, but it hadn't worked.

His smile widened, making her catch her breath. "Can you give me a ride to work?"

"To work?" she echoed foolishly.

He began to walk alongside her toward student parking. "Yeah, it would save me thumbin', and I didn't think you'd mind."

Julie saw three of Angel's friends stop and stare. She squared her shoulders, trying not to grin at the expression on Rudy Juarez's face. Her reputation might be shot if she left school with Angel, but a ruined reputation was a lot more interesting than no reputation at all. Abruptly she thought of what her mother would say if she heard.

"Sure," she found herself answering. "Where do you work?"

He explained as they walked to her car. Julie did her best to ignore the curious stares, but her face was hot. Angel's grin didn't fade until they were out of sight of the two-story school building.

They had almost reached the garage where he worked, neither speaking, when Julie turned a corner and a small dog darted into the road after a cat. She slammed on the brakes as the cat ran into the bush on the other side, unscathed. A sickening thud told Julie the dog hadn't been so lucky.

Shaken, she shifted gears and reached for the door handle. Before she could open it, Angel stopped her with his hand. "No," he said. "Stay in the car while I check."

Julie tried to smile her gratitude, but her lower lip quivered dangerously. Unable to speak, she nodded, blinking rapidly.

Angel stopped at the side of the car and squatted down. In a moment he raised his head. His face was grave. "He's still alive," he said through the open window, "but badly hurt."

* * *

Julie's eyes snapped open at the knock on her bedroom door, and the image of Angel's concerned expression dissolved.

"Julianna, dear," her mother called, "someone's on the phone for you."

Julie got up, smoothing her hair, and opened the door, glancing around the room from long habit. It was neat as a pin, just like she'd been taught. Julie frowned. If she still worried whether her bedroom was tidy enough for her mother, it was time she found a place of her own. As soon as she landed a full-time teaching position, she would.

"Thanks," she said on her way to the phone in the upstairs hallway. "Is it Stef?"

She and Stef had remained friends since high school, even though Stef now worked in the lab at the refinery. She had never married, and Julie hadn't seen much of her friend during her own marriage to Bradley. He'd called Stef "that lesbian" just because she didn't flirt with him, and he had discouraged Julie from seeing her. Now they met for lunch a couple of times a month.

"No, dear. I didn't recognize the voice."

Julie noticed the lines of worry on her mother's forehead. She knew she had disappointed her parents with the failure of her marriage. Without meaning to, she always seemed to disappoint them.

"You should exercise and eat more," her mother said as Julie moved past her. "You haven't been to the pool at the club in months."

Her mother's sigh floated after Julie as she went down the thickly carpeted hallway to the landing at the top of the wide staircase. The caller was Mrs. Hansen from Pinewood Elementary. She had a substitute teaching job available the next day, which Julie eagerly accepted.

From the beginning she had loved teaching, but Bradley had begun voicing his objections right after they married. She'd taught third grade for a year before giving in to his insistence that he needed her to make a home for them, to entertain the right people, to serve on the right committees. After the divorce it had been a while before she had felt up to adding her name to the list of substitute teachers in the district. Now she was glad she had.

Angel pulled his Ferrari into the circular driveway in front of the two-story house he'd bought a few weeks before. He was glad to see his friend Joey's old pickup parked by the triple garage. As Angel got out of the car, one of the darkly polished double front doors of the house was thrown open.

"Angel, my man! I've been waiting for you." Joey came down the steps, hand outstretched.

Angel glanced at it, then pulled his friend into a bear hug. "It's good to see you," he exclaimed as they clapped each other on the back. "Thanks for your help with the house." Joey had been there to take delivery of the furniture Angel bought and sent ahead.

"Hey, man, what else have I got to do?" Joey asked as they broke apart. He'd lost his job when the machining plant on the other side of town had started laying off employees. Unskilled workers like Joey were always the first to go.

Before Angel could reply, a small brown dog came racing across the lawn, barking insistently. It was followed by a high-pitched shout, then a painfully thin woman wearing a mauve suit and matching shoes hurried toward them.

"I'm so sorry," she said breathlessly, scooping up the yapping dog. "Baby got loose." She looked suspiciously from one man to the other, frowning. Then recognition dawned, and she smiled at Angel and jabbed a manicured finger under his nose.

"I know who you are. I saw your picture in the paper. You're that famous race car driver, Antonio something."

Angel glanced past her shoulder at Joey, who was grinning. "Angel Maneros," he corrected. "And this is my friend Joey Lopez." He wondered idly if thinking of him as an Italian made his presence in the exclusive neighborhood more acceptable.

"Gilda Hildabrandt," she supplied, staring into his face. "Maneros, did you say?"

He nodded.

Mrs. Hildabrandt inclined her head, but didn't offer her hand. "Pleased to meet you." She glanced at Joey's tank top and worn jeans, then back at Angel's more expensive bleached denims and chambray shirt. "Excuse me, it's time for Baby's bath."

As she hurried back to the large Tudor house next door, Angel pulled a canvas bag from the car and walked up the front steps.

"You ruined her day, man," Joey said behind him. "She's probably wondering right now when you're going to start parking beat-up old cars on the front lawn."

Angel grinned over his shoulder, not stopping until he was standing in the tiled entryway. He'd dreamed of owning a house like this someday, but Julie had always been in the picture with him. Instead no one was here to see his triumph except his old buddy.

He continued through the house as his friend unloaded the other suitcase from the car. The little dog, Baby, had reminded him of another, less fortunate little brown dog whose name he had never learned. Returning to Clarkson had filled his head with memories, and to this day he could remember clearly the expression on Julie's face when he'd told her the dog was badly hurt.

As Angel bent over the injured animal, Julianna got out of the car, pulling off her fuzzy white cardigan. "I'll take him to the vet," she said, looking down at the dog. She thrust the sweater at Angel. "Cover him with this."

His hands closed on the incredibly soft garment. "You sure?"

"Yes. Please hurry." Her voice shook.

She twisted her hands together while he carefully wrapped up the trembling little dog and lifted him slowly. Except for one brief whine, the animal didn't bark or growl, although it was obvious he was in pain.

Straightening, Angel glanced at Julianna. She looked like she was in pain herself. Her skin was pale and her eyes huge. A girl like her had probably never seen death, Angel thought. He felt a pang of pity as he slid onto the seat. Already there was a smear of blood on his white T-shirt.

"There's no tag," he said as she got behind the wheel. "I wonder if he lives around here."

She looked at the dog, whose eyes were closed. "Should we try to find his owner?"

"No, he could die while we look." He cursed himself silently as she turned even paler. "You know a vet?" he asked quickly.

Pulling back onto the road, she nodded. "I'll drop you at work first," she said. "It's only two blocks."

"Don't talk crazy. I'll go with you."

Julianna hesitated. "You'll be late."

"Naw. I got two hours before I start."

If she wondered at his request for a ride, she didn't comment, watching the road as she headed back into the middle of town. The little dog whined again, shuddering in the soft cocoon of Julianna's sweater. Angel hoped for her sake that it would pull through.

"Hang on, *amigo*," he murmured a few moments later, placing a quieting hand on the dog's head as Julianna parked the car before a dark red building with white shutters.

"You got any money with you?" Angel asked her.

Julianna frowned. "Money?"

He rubbed his thumb across his fingers in a circular motion. "You know, that green stuff that you swap for things."

"I have twenty dollars in my purse. Why?"

"These guys won't talk to you without cash up front."

Her expression cleared. "Oh, don't worry," she said. "My parents have an account here. Dr. Roberts takes care of Dad's hunting dogs and Mother's Persian cat."

"Oh yeah, his hunting dogs," Angel muttered to himself as he carefully slid from the car, trying not to jar his burden.

After Julianna had explained what had happened, the receptionist showed Angel into an examining room, where he gently set the little dog on the table.

"Dr. Roberts will be right in," she said, shutting the door behind them.

While they waited, anxiously watching the animal, Julianna touched Angel's bare arm. When he met her eyes, she gave him one of those hesitant little smiles that warmed him more than the other girls' flirtatious smirks.

"I owe you another one," she said. "Thank you again."

Her quiet words made him shift uncomfortably. "It's nothin'," he said impatiently. "I didn't have anything better to do."

Her smile faded, and he frowned at the harsh way he'd spoken. This whole thing obviously had upset her, and he wasn't helping any. He cast about for something else to say, but the door opened, admitting an older man in a white coat. He barely acknowledged the two of them before turning his attention to the dog.

After a moment the vet suggested that Julianna and Angel return to the waiting room. While they sat there, Angel found himself trying to make conversation to take Julianna's mind off what was happening inside. A half hour went by before Dr. Roberts came out, his face serious.

"I'm sorry, but he didn't make it. The internal damage was too great."

Julianna stiffened, and a low moan worked its way up from her throat. It seemed only natural for her to turn blindly toward Angel, eyes swimming with tears, and for him to take her into his arms and do his best to comfort her.

Joey came into the large kitchen where Angel was leaning against a center island, staring into space.

"Pretty fancy," he remarked, looking at the expanse of cabinets and counter. "Can you cook?"

Angel laughed shortly. "If I couldn't cook, I would have starved a long time ago. Did you think I could always afford to eat in restaurants on the circuit?"

Joey shrugged. "I didn't figure you'd have much trouble finding a willing señorita to fry your tortillas," he said. "Back in high school even the rich chicks swarmed around you like flies."

Angel noticed his friend's envious tone but chose to ignore it. He'd gotten away from the town and made a success of his life, and there would be many of his old friends who were jealous, but he'd worked hard, and taken chances that others weren't willing to risk. And he'd been lucky, which was more than he could say for Bill Patch, the driver who had been killed during Angel's last race.

"You'll be okay," he said to Joey. "Whatever happened to Maria, anyway?"

Joey turned his back and looked out the window. "She went to school and got a hairdresser's license. Married some white dude down in Bellevue."

For a moment Angel was silent. Maria and Joey had been inseparable during high school, but she'd broken off with him when he quit. "Well," Angel said heartily, "I bet there have been plenty of other women since Maria."

Joey turned. "Yeah, man. Plenty. But I guess we both had someone who got away. Julie married another dude, too."

Joey had been the one to tell Angel of her marriage, remarking at the time that it didn't surprise him.

Angel clenched his fists at his sides. He still remembered the gut-twisting pain he'd felt at Joey's words. He should have known she wouldn't wait. To hear that she'd married some hotshot lawyer whose family came from the hill had turned him inside out at the time, but it was after that that his career really soared as he began to take chances, pushing himself and his cars to the limit. His exploits off the track made headlines, too. Obviously what he and Julie once shared had only been a teenage crush to her, a temporary detour from the path she'd been born to.

Angel heard the phone ringing in another part of the house as Joey left the room. After a moment, he returned.

"Hey, man, Mrs. Phoebe Moneybags Remington is on the phone, and she wants to talk to you," he said in a poor imitation of a snooty accent.

Julie's mother.

Chapter Two

Angel frowned as he put the receiver to his ear. "Hello?" His voice was unnecessarily forceful to hide his inner hesitation. What on earth could Julie's mother want with him?

"Mr. Maneros, I realize you're barely settled, and I apologize for disturbing you," Phoebe Remington said softly, "but I wanted to invite you to the hospital fundraiser my guild is having at the country club this weekend."

Angel's dark brows drew together as he waited for her to continue. After a brief hesitation, Mrs. Remington gave her pitch, explaining how much good the guild had done for the local hospital over the years. He wondered how much of that good extended to the less fortunate members of the community.

"Can we count on you to be there?" she asked when he still didn't speak.

Angel mulled the idea over quickly. Undoubtedly there would be people there he needed to meet if he wanted to get his own plans off the ground. He knew that he'd been invited for his drawing power as a celebrity and because Mrs. Remington hoped to get a big check from him.

"Thank you," he said into the phone, breaking the silence that was beginning to stretch past tolerable lengths. "I'd be delighted to attend."

"Wonderful. Oh, one last thing. The dinner will be black tie. That means—"

"I know what it means," he said, interrupting the flow of her words.

"Of course you do," she said smoothly. "I won't keep you, but we are all looking forward to seeing you Saturday evening."

Angel was tempted to ask if that included her daughter, but before he could form the words, Mrs. Remington had hung up. How would Julie feel about seeing him again? Did she regret what had happened, or had she been relieved when it was all over between them? Had she ever told her parents? She'd been so afraid they would find out and keep her and Angel apart during high school. Wouldn't her society old lady have been thrilled to learn her only daughter was going with a nobody like him?

He shook his head, banishing the questions. He couldn't let his thoughts run down that familiar path again. It only led to aching uncertainty and almost unbearable torment. He must remember that Julie had simply changed her mind. He had to leave the memory in the past where it belonged.

Angel slammed down the receiver he still held in a choking grip. Julie had realized how much she would be giving up for him, and the sacrifice had been too great. After he left to find some kind of future, she had resumed the normal pattern of her life and forgotten all about him. The rational side of him had long since realized she had probably done both of them a big favor.

Still, the idea of seeing her in her native setting, on her husband's arm, made Angel's stomach knot with unexpected pain.

"Damn you, Julie!" he exclaimed, driving a fist into the wood of the doorjamb. The dull thud brought Joey running.

"What's wrong?" he asked. "What did that woman want?"

Angel frowned uncomprehendingly, cradling his stinging knuckles. For a moment he'd even forgotten Joey's presence in the large house.

"Nothing. Nothing's wrong," he insisted in answer to Joey, who was staring as if Angel had grown a second head. "I have to wear a tux to a fancy charity dinner Saturday, and I hate climbing into those monkey suits."

After a moment Joey shook his head, turning away. "Yeah, it's a rough life," he said over his shoulder. Angel heard him mumble something else as he moved down the hall.

As Angel walked into the huge rec room at the back of the house, staring across the pool table to the wide view of the golf course, he realized how grateful he was for Joey's company. Angel had been relieved when the other man had accepted his offer of employment. Joey had his pride and insisted that it was only until something permanent came along. He'd been a great help opening up the house and stocking it with groceries. Angel had tried to tell Joey how valuable he was, but he couldn't shake Joey of the idea that working for Angel was accepting charity.

Joey would do the cooking and keep up the outside of the house, answer the phone and run errands. His cousin Consuela would be coming in twice a week to clean. The arrangement would give Angel more time to get started with his plans and give Joey some income. Soon Angel's half brother Luis would be released from prison, and he, too, would be joining them. Angel hoped his friend didn't find a permanent job too soon.

The night of the hospital benefit, Julie was in her room glaring at the pile of dresses that spilled across her bed as riotously as an explosion in a flower shop. She'd lost weight, since the divorce, that she had only recently begun to regain, and they were all too big. Her extremely slim figure would fit right in with the fashion-conscious crowd attending the dinner dance that evening. The saying that one could never be too rich or too thin could have been the official motto for some members of the wealthy set, of which her parents were the acknowledged leaders.

Julie's hair had been trimmed so it waved away from her face, the back hanging past her shoulders. The strands at her temples had been lightly frosted to brighten the medium brown color she had always considered unbearably ordinary, and her nails were freshly done in a luminescent pearl beige. She'd been fitted for contact lenses back in college and still considered her hazel eyes the best feature in an insignificant face.

Julie had never understood what attracted Angel to her, but she'd been too wrapped up in him to dwell on it. Ever since that day at the vet's when Angel had drawn her into his comforting embrace, something wonderful had grown steadily between them. Angel had consoled her then, listening patiently as she poured out her unhappiness, first about the dog's death, then about so many other things. When she had finally faltered to a stop he had, even more amazingly, shared some of his own thoughts and feelings with her.

That day they became friends—mismatched, incongruous, but friends all the same. A bond had formed, one they both silently acknowledged. In the days that followed, they managed to see each other often, during and after school. The talk that buzzed around them bothered neither. Angel ignored it, and Julie was too happy to be aware of it until her best friend Stef finally confronted her.

Stef was the only one to whom Julie told the truth. By then she loved Angel as only a sixteen-year-old can. Stef's initial reaction was fear that Julie would be hurt.

But she was already hurting for Angel because he had to live with poverty and the hateful prejudice that came his way every day—prejudice over things he hadn't chosen and couldn't change.

Deliberately banishing the painful memories, the grown-up Julie twirled in front of the full-length mirror, studying her cream silk dress with a critical eye. It depended on faultless tailoring and a wide gold belt to make it dressy enough for the dance. With its calf-length skirt she wore cream stockings and matching suede shoes. The dress's shirtwaist style flattered her figure, and the color played up the highlights in her hair.

She wondered what Angel would think, if he would remember the other dance they'd attended. They had met at the high school gym, trying to appear casual as they floated in each other's arms, Julie in a winter-white semiformal, Angel in an ill-fitting rented tux.

She suspected he would remember the fight afterward, even if he had forgotten the events that were etched so clearly into her own mind. He'd gotten a black eye and skinned knuckles when three football players made unflattering remarks about Julie's choice of a companion. None of Angel's friends had attended the dance, but they'd materialized outside the gym as if by magic to even the odds before two teachers intervened. Only Julie's support had saved Angel from a suspension at the time.

Now, as she picked through her tray of earrings in search of her gold and pearl hoops, she couldn't help but wonder how the people who had been so quick to condemn him would feel when they had to shake his hand and welcome him back to town. Her own mother had certainly moved quickly enough in inviting him to this bash at the country club. Julie knew she hoped to get a big contribution for her pet charity, the new children's wing.

When she had told Julie of the coup, it reminded her of the remark her mother had made when she'd picked Julie up at school early one cold afternoon. Several of Angel's friends were hanging around outside, waiting for the closing bell.

"Look at those ruffians," Mrs. Remington had said. "Too lazy to stay in school. They'll end up doing seasonal work if they're lucky, and having huge families our taxes will pay for."

At the time Julie had thought of Angel and kept silent. Her mother would never understand.

Now, not for the first time since Julie had heard the news, she wondered why he was back. As she was trying to fasten one earring, it dawned on her that Brad, her ex-husband, would probably be at the dance, too. He'd called several times when she first left him, but she hadn't seen him for quite a while. For her, any emotional ties had been severed long before the divorce itself.

Now Brad was dating Heather Bates, and when Julie had first heard, she'd been torn between warning the other girl and gloating. Heather had been a member of the exclusive clique who'd tormented and snubbed Julie during high school, the clique Julie's parents had wanted so badly for her to join.

She bent down to search the thick carpet for the earring back she'd dropped, almost wishing she could stay home. Having to face both Brad and Angel on the same night was not a pleasant proposition.

Finally she found what she was looking for and finished putting in the hoops with shaking fingers. Painful as it would undoubtedly be, seeing Angel again when they were both surrounded by other people might prove to be the best way. Pride would keep her from demanding answers to the questions that had buzzed in her head like angry bees when he'd gone away after swearing he couldn't leave without her.

She studied her reflection in the mirror, pleased with the way she had changed from the skinny kid in glasses he'd known in high school to someone who was reasonably attractive, with the right hairstyle and clothes. Even her current thinness only accentuated her cheekbones and made her eyes look larger. She would let Angel see what he'd abandoned, and then she would cut him dead. As for Brad, she almost felt that he and Heather deserved each other.

* * *

Angel arrived late, standing in the doorway of the huge room and watching the other guests fill their plates from the sumptuous buffet set up along one wall. Small round tables and white, wrought iron chairs framed the large dance floor. A band onstage was playing something slow.

Angel had been telling the truth when he told Joey he hated wearing formal dress, but he was well aware of the impression he made. He couldn't have picked a better first meeting with Julie, he thought, remembering the rented tux he'd been forced to wear one night long ago after the clerk insisted Angel's order had been misplaced. That jacket had been too short and too big around, but this sleek garment was custom-tailored to his height and the width of his shoulders. It felt almost as good as leather and denim.

"Excuse me," an older man said as Angel surveyed the crowd. "I saw you win at Indy two years ago, and I just wanted to tell you how impressed I was. Great driving."

Angel returned the man's smile, trying to place the familiar face. "Mr. Thomas?" he questioned.

The man flushed with pleasure and stuck out a hand. "Didn't think you'd remember."

"How could I forget the shop teacher who taught me so much about engines? It's nice to see you again, but what are you doing here?" Then Angel realized what he'd said and shook his head ruefully. "I meant—"

"What's a junior high teacher doing at a country club dance," the older man filled in, grinning at Angel's discomfort. "I'm the principal now, and the hospital's new wing is a favorite project of mine."

Angel stuck out his hand again. "Congratulations. I hadn't heard."

They talked for a few more minutes before George Thomas excused himself. He'd been one of a handful of teachers who had seemed to care about Angel as a student, and who had encouraged him to stay in school.

Angel's eyes narrowed and his body went rigid as his gaze locked with that of a woman across the room. Tension twisted through him, followed by a longing so strong and so raw that it shocked him. Before he could force his legs to obey his urgent command to carry him in her direction, another man involved him in a round of introductions. By the time Angel managed to extricate himself, the woman had disappeared.

One glimpse of the tall, dark man standing just inside the wide doorway was enough to send Julie hurrying back toward the bar that had been set up in the corner. Her breath had snagged in her lungs, and her heart seemed to be blocking her throat, threatening to choke her. She'd already consumed one vodka and tonic as she kept up a nervous surveillance of the new arrivals. Usually she didn't drink, except for a glass of wine with dinner, but tonight she needed extra fortification, she told herself as she wrapped her fingers around a second glass. She held it tightly as she skirted the crowd, searching for Angel's dark head above the masses, but she failed to spot him. Whirling quickly, she plowed into a muscular chest, splaying the fingers of her free hand across a snowy shirtfront as two deeply tanned hands gripped her upper arms.

"Easy," cautioned a heartbreakingly familiar voice as Julie stared hard at a black pearl stud, swallowing past the sudden dryness in her throat.

As she tilted back her chin, her gaze flew to the blue eyes she'd once known so well. They seemed to burn with a cold flame. She couldn't keep herself from examining the rest of Angel's face, noticing with a burst of mingled pride and regret that maturity had turned a handsome boy into a devastatingly attractive man. Then she saw the disdainful smile that curved his beautiful mouth, and her blood turned to ice.

Strained nerves forced a careless laugh past her stiff lips.

"The conquering hero returns," she babbled, needing desperately to fill the silence between them. "What brings you back to our little burg, Mr. Racing Driver Maneros?" She noticed through her panic that his hands squeezed her painfully before they dropped to his sides.

"Unfinished business," he said, his voice deeper but as velvety as her memories. Angel's glittering gaze narrowed. "Where's your husband?" His mouth formed the word with obvious distaste.

The question surprised her. "You mean Brad?"

"How many husbands do you have?"

She wanted to tell him she didn't have any, but the realization that he'd apparently heard about her marriage and not her divorce stilled her tongue. The charade, no matter how brief, would give her time to compose her suddenly shattered nerves. She gazed around the room slowly, trying to still her quaking body. Her hands were shaking, and she gripped her full glass harder.

"I don't see him," she answered in what she hoped was a calm tone. Her heart was beating so loudly she was surprised that Angel couldn't seem to hear it.

Angel's hands clamped down on her shoulders, the heat from his palms soaking through the thin material and burning her. "Are you happy?" he demanded as she forced herself not to flinch from his touch.

Julie barely resisted the wild laughter that rose to her lips. Happy? Had she felt true happiness since he'd left? Her life had taken a disastrous turn that she was only now able to put behind her, while Angel's seemed to have been blessed by all the saints in his religion.

Her head bobbed in answer to his question. "I've been very happy." He frowned darkly, releasing her, and her gaze slid away from his as she pretended to scan the crowd.

Before Angel could ask another question, two men who had obviously spent considerable time at the bar came up, demanding loudly that he settle a dispute about one of his races. As he turned to deal with them, Julie slipped away.

She headed straight for the ladies' lounge, depositing her unwanted drink on a passing tray as she went. Luckily the lounge was deserted, and she sank into a maroon velvet chair with a sigh of relief, gulping in deep, calming breaths. Her pulses were tripping along in overdrive, and her heart felt as if it would explode in her chest. All the reaction she'd managed to repress when she had been talking to Angel poured forth. Her nails dug into the arms of the velvet chair, and her vision blurred and focused inward.

The last ten years had changed Angel, maturing him and hardening his thin, handsome face. The blue eyes that had gazed upon her with tenderness and affection so long ago, now glinted with a cold light that chilled her, cooling her initial heated reaction to his dark attractiveness and the male power of his tall, muscular frame.

The tux he wore tonight was every bit as compelling as the tight jeans and scarred leather jacket she remembered so well. His black hair, once long and carelessly trimmed, was now expensively styled. It was still longer than was currently fashionable, sweeping back from his forehead and brushing his collar, but now no red bandanna held it in place.

Julie was swamped with regrets and burning, unanswered questions. Why had he gone, after he'd sworn on his mother's memory that he couldn't survive without her? And why did he have to return now, when she was beginning to pick up the pieces of her own devastated life?

Only a deep instinct for emotional survival enabled Julie to face the rest of the evening. She worked her way back to the large room, chin thrust determinedly forward, knowing it would be just her luck to have to suffer not only Angel's disturbing presence but that of her ex-husband as well. The thought was enough to make her press her evening bag protectively against her heart, in much the same way she'd held her schoolbooks years before.

Angel had been busy while Julie was gone, trying to get a look at her husband. The knife-sharp pain that had sliced into his gut when he first looked into her face had receded only slightly, and now morbid curiosity drove him to see who had succeeded where Angel himself had failed—in getting Julie to trust herself and her future to someone else. When yet another racing fan pointed Bradley Hammond out to him, Angel was surprised to see one of his own former classmates at the other man's side, her arm linked possessively through his.

Angel had run in some pretty sophisticated circles during his career, but it had never occurred to him that anyone fortunate enough to marry Julie would bother with other women. As Angel watched, frowning blackly, Hammond and his companion disappeared through one of the French doors leading to the garden outside. Silently Angel followed.

When Julie returned she was relieved to see that both of the men she wanted to avoid had disappeared. Instead her mother beckoned to her from a nearby knot of people. Julie crossed over to them.

"Julianna, dear, you remember the Simpsons from Bellevue. They were up for the golf tournament and barbecue last summer."

"Of course. Nice to see you both again." Neither face looked the least bit familiar to her.

After brief pleasantries were exchanged, Mr. Simpson resumed a story he'd been telling about the sixth hole at Pebble Beach. Julie glanced nervously over her shoulder, beginning to feel uncomfortably warm in the crowded room. The emotions dredged up during her encounter with Angel had sapped her energy, and a headache hovered just beyond the edges of her consciousness.

"Darling, are you feeling all right?" her mother asked quietly. "You've gone quite pale."

Grateful that her mother had no clue as to the turmoil Angel's return had brought her, Julie summoned up a smile. "I think a little fresh air will do the trick. I'll see you later."

"Bradley hasn't bothered you, has he?" Her mother's voice was sharper. After the divorce, when Julie had confided why she'd left, both of her parents had been wonderfully supportive. Her mother especially had been horrified to hear of Brad's drunken rages. And her father had wanted to press charges when he saw the marks on Julie's neck. Interested only in being completely free of the marriage that had soured long before, she had talked him out of it.

Now Julie patted the hand her mother had laid on her arm. "I haven't even seen him this evening."

"Oh, he's here. With that social-climbing little twit he's been dating."

Julie smiled to hear her mother's description of Heather Bates. And to think Julie had once been under the impression her mother wanted her to be more like the other woman. Glad she hadn't touched that second drink, Julie excused herself and headed outside.

There were several couples in the shadows, and she began to feel self-conscious, so after a few minutes she turned to go back inside. As she did, a familiar voice called her name, sending an unpleasant chill down her spine. Bravely she turned to face her ex-husband and his current flame, who were standing on the shallow steps of a patio ringed with bushes.

"Alone, Julianna?" Brad asked with a sneer. He'd hooked an arm around Heather, who was looking at Julie with a pitying expression.

"Only momentarily," Julie returned with a lift of her chin. "I've been recovering from a bad marriage and a messy divorce, but I'm finally cured of it, and you."

Brad's mocking grin turned sour. "I heard you went back home to Mommy and Daddy. A good place for a spoiled infant."

Julie grew taut at his unprovoked attack and had to hold her temper in severe check. "You're the one who spoiled me, in ways we don't need to discuss now. I really hope you get some help, Brad, before you try again."

There was a small satisfaction in the way his smoothly handsome face flushed in the dim light. Next to him, Heather opened her mouth to protest, but Julie raised a detaining hand. "Take care, Heather. I'm telling you for your own good, he's not what he seems."

Brad advanced threateningly, features twisted with anger. "Watch your vicious tongue, bitch, or I'll sue you for slander," he growled, waving a clenched fist beneath her nose.

Cold fear shuddered through Julie, but before she could think of a reply, a tall figure stepped from the darkness of the surrounding bushes.

"Back away," the man said in a menacing voice, "or you'll be suing me instead. For assault with intent to do serious bodily harm."

Julie gasped at Angel's sudden appearance, realizing almost instantly that he must have heard every word that had been spoken. Her hopes for a temporary charade were shattered.

Brad stared at Angel, his face mottled with anger. For a moment his struggle for control was obvious, then he managed a haughty smile as he turned to Heather and offered his arm.

"Would you care for dessert now?" he asked as if the ugly scene had never taken place. Only a familiar tremor in Brad's voice betrayed the fury that Julie knew still gripped him. Heather's head bobbed in agreement as she took his arm and they swept past, giving Angel a wide berth. Julie's gaze followed them for a moment before she turned to the man who stood beside her. He was clearly as tense as a snake waiting to strike.

"That wasn't necessary." Her knees were knocking together, and she had to fight the urge to fling herself into his arms.

"It sounded like it to me. He was threatening you, and he called you a name I've fought over before."

Julie remembered an altercation in the high school parking lot. Angel had gotten a bloody nose for defending her reputation, but the other boy had fared much worse.

"I've been fighting my own battles for quite some time now," she said, a hint of bitterness in her tone.

"Why didn't you tell me that you're no longer married?" Angel demanded, his deep voice raising goose bumps on her arms.

"I hate to think of myself as a divorced woman. It reeks of failure."

His gaze was intense, and his black brows pulled into a frown as he studied her. "Not good enough. Why did you want me to think you still have a husband?" A muscle in his cheek twitched, and his teeth were a pale slash in the dark menace of his face.

She stepped back. He'd changed in more than just appearance. The tenderness he'd always shown her had been replaced by a primitive male power that frightened her more than Brad's ugly temper.

"Why should I try to explain? Just when and how was I supposed to let you know?" Her own voice was filled with the anger of years. "We were hardly pen pals."

Looking down into her face, Angel forced himself to relax, raking long fingers through his hair. "I had heard that you married," he said, fighting the pain the words revived in his gut. "But I didn't know that you had ended it. What happened?"

Julie's eyes widened and her delicate brows rose. "None of your business," she snapped. "Why have you come back?"

"I could answer you with the same words," he drawled, unable to resist the urge to bait her. She began to turn away, and he wanted desperately to keep her with him for a few moments more.

"Wait. I'll answer your question."

She stopped, eyeing him curiously, but didn't speak.

"I'm here to set up a center for the Chicanos." To his ears the words sounded self-important and conceited. He sighed and slid a hand into his pocket, reaching for the cigarettes he'd given up months before. Who was he to take on a project as vital as this one?

It was obvious he'd sparked her curiosity. "What kind of center?" she asked.

"Day-care, some classes on nutrition and budgeting. Later, perhaps a clinic and a gift shop to sell handicrafts. Whatever we decide they need the most, I guess. I want to pattern it on some of the places I saw in California. Also I've been thinking of offering adult literacy classes, and eventually some job placement help."

He *was* planning to stay for good, Julie thought, not sure how the news made her feel. "They have a reading course for adults at the community college," she said. She had taken the training course to be a tutor but had never used it.

"How many of the Chicanos you know go to the community college?"

"I don't know."

"Not very damned many, I'll bet," he replied grimly.

She stared into the face that was the best possible mix of two bloodlines, noticing the way the dim light emphasized his strong cheekbones and the hollows beneath them. Her gaze skimmed down his straight, slender nose and rested on his mouth. A tremor shook her. She remembered the touch of those lips more clearly than the taste of the coffee she'd had that morning, much more clearly than her husband's touch months before. The memory of Angel's kisses would haunt her forever.

"Will you be working with some state agency?" she asked, trying to blot out the way he affected her.

"No. Too much red tape, too much control. This will belong to the people, funded by private donations, I hope."

And he'd pour his own money and sweat into it, she thought, recalling how caring, how generous he could be. Remember the pain, she instructed herself, not the good parts. Remember the desertion. And the years of silence.

"What about you?" he asked after a moment. "Do you work?"

"I'm a teacher," she said proudly, then remembered that she hadn't yet found a full-time job. "I'm substituting right now, but I expect to have something permanent very soon." She flushed in the dimness. "A permanent teaching position," she added quickly, lest he think she was hinting for a job.

He saw her glance at the brightly lit windows and filed away the information she had just given him. "Do you want to go back inside?" he asked, looking for a reason to keep her with him. "Would you like to dance?"

The expression on her face changed abruptly. "Not with you!" she said bluntly. Her eyes blazed. "Never with you."

As she whirled and hurried through the open doors, Angel jammed his hands deep into his pockets to keep himself from smashing them against the low concrete wall. Her rejection of his offer sent pain slicing through him with all the finesse of a chain saw. If he had thought for a fleeting moment that there could be anything between them again, he'd been wrong. Even though she was divorced, the fury he saw in her eyes had been unmistakable. She hated him.

Angel's shoulders drooped slightly as he made his way around the outside of the building to the parking lot. He'd heard that tone and seen that scornful expression many times before, but he'd never expected to hear and see it from the one woman who'd taken his heart so long ago and never returned it.

Perhaps coming back to town had been a big mistake. Who had he been kidding when he told himself it was only to set up the center? Deep down he'd never really accepted Julie's change of heart, but now it was clearly time to rid himself of any lingering hopes for the two of them. Too much time had passed.

Julie was lost to him forever, just as her sweet, shining innocence was apparently lost even to herself. The woman he'd encountered tonight still intrigued and attracted him, but his sense of self-preservation was too strong to let him knock on locked doors. Better to accept that the love he'd shared with Julie as a teenager was gone too long ago to ever recapture. Maybe she had done the right thing when she had refused to run away with him, after all.

He slid behind the wheel of his Ferrari. For a long moment he stared sightlessly through the windshield.

"Damn you, Julianna," he muttered through gritted teeth as his fist slammed against the steering wheel. "Damn you."

He shook his head to clear it. Then he started the Ferrari and roared from the parking lot, leaving a large chunk of emotions he refused to examine too closely behind in a cloud of dust.

Julie's encounter with Angel had shattered the walls she'd built around herself and her feelings since the divorce. No longer was she able to blank out the pain and disappointment her marriage to Brad had brought, or its final, violent ending. No longer could she shove the image of Angel from her mind's eye when he intruded.

She called Stef and made plans to meet for lunch, she talked to Mrs. Hansen to see if there were any more substitute teaching jobs coming up soon and she thought seriously about volunteering her services at the hospital. Before she actually got around to signing up, the day of her luncheon date with Stef came.

Her friend was already seated in a booth at their favorite restaurant when Julie arrived, feeling slightly self-conscious in a new dress and shoes. Yesterday she'd gone to one of the big malls on the way to Seattle and bought several outfits that didn't hang so loosely on her slim frame.

"Wow!" Stef exclaimed when Julie slid in across from her. "Did you forget it was me you were meeting? You look like you expected some movie star. I like the dress, though."

Julie smiled sheepishly and glanced at the oversized beige sweater her friend was wearing. "I've been looking forward to our lunch," she said, wishing that Stef would pay closer attention to her own appearance. Julie knew her friend was interested in a man at the refinery, but in her white lab coat, with her straight blond hair scraped back and no makeup, she'd never be noticed as anything but a fellow employee.

"Been shopping?" Stef persisted, leaning forward to study the dress's silky fabric.

"Uh-huh." Julie read her menu with great interest.

"This wouldn't have anything to do with the return to town of a certain celebrity ex-classmate, would it?" Stef asked.

Julie's head jerked up and she frowned. "Of course not. Can't I buy a few clothes that fit without you—"

Stef held up her hands in self-defense. "Whoa. Of course you can. Let's order, and then you can tell me about the dance at the country club. Was he there?"

Julie ignored the question, continuing to study her menu diligently. After they'd given the waitress their choices, Stef sat back expectantly and stared. Julie shifted uncomfortably and sipped from her water glass.

"How did he look?" Stef finally asked. "Anything like he did in that poster that sold a million copies?"

"At the dance he was wearing a tux." Julie remembered the poster. It had shattered sales records, and her copy was rolled up and shoved into the back of her closet at home.

Angel had been standing lazily in a doorway, his bare, broad chest gleaming with the rich, mellow glow of oiled wood. One thumb was hitched casually into the waistband of jeans that rode ridiculously low, jeans that fit his male body like a lover's hands. His piercing blue eyes and half smile sent a mixed message of welcome and warning, leaving the viewer unsure if she should advance with care or run like hell. The poster's success had led him to a lucrative contract with a top cosmetic company and exclusive promotion of a men's cologne named "Dark Angel," which was expensive, classy and immensely popular.

"If you'd rather not discuss it . . ." Stef's voice was tinged with disappointment. She might deliberately egg Julie out of a moody spell, but she would never pry.

Julie sighed. She needed to talk to someone, and Stef was the only person who knew the whole story about Angel and herself. Well, almost the whole story.

Julie shrugged and proceeded to fill her friend in on the events of the Saturday evening before.

Chapter Three

You must have known you couldn't keep your divorce a secret from Angel forever," Stef said.

Julie nodded. "I just didn't expect him to find out quite so quickly. I wanted more time to adjust to his being back first." She didn't add that her attempted charade was unnecessary, since Angel wasn't interested in her. His face had been frozen into an expression of chilling disapproval.

Stef reached across the table and patted Julie's hand, pulling back as the waitress set down their sandwiches and salads. Both women remained silent until she left.

"You said he doesn't care about you anymore, but he did intervene with Brad, and he asked you to dance," Stef remarked.

"And he left me ten years ago and never wrote," Julie added, not even trying to keep the bitterness from her voice. "He didn't have to enlist in the army right before graduation, and he would have stayed in touch if he cared half as much as I did.''

She'd been shattered to learn that Angel had gone ahead and left town alone. When the months crept by with no word from him, she'd realized how badly he had misunderstood her change of heart. Now it was too late. Ten years too late.

"What you're saying might be true," Stef said. "Maybe he should have stayed in touch. But would you have stayed if the situation was reversed and he had been the one to back out?''

"I did it for us. I never dreamed he'd leave anyway. I planned to see him later, to explain." Julie clenched her hands together tightly in her lap. "I suffered for it," she said in a low voice.

"You carried a torch all through college."

Julie's eyes were filled with pain. "At first I thought he'd contact me when he was stationed somewhere. But he began winning races before I was even sure he had been discharged, and still I never heard. And then my parents were so disappointed when I majored in education instead of something more prestigious, that when they started to hint that a marriage with Brad would make them happy..." Her throat tightened and she took another sip of water.

"I saw those pictures of Angel with that beauty queen from South Carolina all over him like cheap wallpaper," she continued, "and there didn't seem to be any point in waiting. Brad was eager enough to marry me, and I thought we could make it work.''

"We all know what a bad idea that was," Stef interjected. "Still, how could you know he had a drinking problem and an uncontrollable temper, when all he let you see was his smarmy charm?" Stef shuddered. She had never liked Brad and made no attempt to hide her feelings.

"But it was my own fault that it took three years to leave him," Julie said. "My parents never knew about the fights until after I filed for divorce."

"Then they finally decided their darling daughter hadn't screwed up again," Stef added dryly. The Remingtons' lack of support during Julie's separation was a sore point with her.

"They're helping me now," Julie said, glancing at the clock before biting into her sandwich. Stef only had an hour for lunch before she had to be back at work. "They've given me a place to stay, and they never knew till the end that Brad had been physical with his anger."

"Letting you move back home was a mixed blessing. Sometimes I've thought you needed a swift kick to get you going again, and I'm glad you finally climbed out of that hole you were digging."

Julie's eyebrows rose at her friend's blunt words.

"I think Angel's story about opening a center for Chicanos is only a cover," Stef said, changing the subject as she picked up a cherry tomato from her salad. "Don't forget, I saw you two together in high school. I knew then he loved you, and I can't believe he's been able to turn it off completely. There has to be more there than his macho pride, and I'm sure if you try, you can explain to him why you didn't show up. After all, you were only kids then."

Julie shook her head, color flooding her cheeks when she remembered just what had happened the last time she saw him before he left town. She'd played what she thought then was her last ace to keep him in Clarkson.

"He has no feelings left and neither do I. He swore he couldn't leave without me, and the next thing I knew he was gone."

She chose to ignore the fact that she had been the one to back out at the very last minute, going to a brunch with her parents instead of meeting Angel to run away with him. She'd only done it because she had sincerely believed they would both be better off staying in Clarkson, at least until they graduated. How could two teenagers have hoped to make a life together based on love alone?

Angel had sworn that he would take care of her, but Julie had always been afraid she would only hold him back, despite the deep feelings she had for him. Too many obstacles had loomed ahead. So when her parents had suggested she accompany them to a brunch that morning, it had been almost a relief to acquiesce, as if fate were giving her a way out. Later, when Angel had called, when she had told him she wasn't going, it had felt like her very soul was being torn from her. His disbelief and hurt had sliced her to ribbons, but she'd clung to her decision. For him, her heart cried. She'd done it for him.

Stef's expression was obstinate. "Angel Maneros did come back, though, because he still wants you. If he didn't care, he'd have a wife and kids by now. He was always big on family."

Julie chewed the suddenly tasteless roast beef and thought about what Stef had said. When she and Angel had been meeting privately during his senior year, they had spent a lot of time talking. They'd shared their dreams and made plans to marry someday and have a lot of children. She knew how important that was to the man who'd had only a mother and a convict half brother to claim as relatives. Perhaps Stef had a point.

No, she couldn't let herself think that way. Ten years of silence proved her friend wrong.

"I never knew you were such a romantic," she said lightly. "It must be that new man at work who's mellowed your hard heart."

Stef flushed, and toyed with her fork. "I wonder if Angel's brother is out of prison yet," she said after a moment. "What was he in for, anyway?"

It was obvious to Julie that Stef wasn't ready to discuss the fellow employee who'd caught her interest several weeks before. Not wanting to push, even though Stef had been outspoken about Angel, she went along with the change of subject.

"I think Luis was in for armed robbery. Angel hardly ever talked about him, although he mentioned once that they'd been close when Angel was little, and that he didn't believe Luis was guilty. I don't remember how long the sentence was, but he'd only been sent up the year before we met."

"He couldn't have been very old."

"Eight years older than Angel, and only a half brother, don't forget." Angel's mother hadn't been married to the fathers of either of her children. She had worked in a bar at the other end of town when Julie was in high school, and she'd been killed accidentally during a fight there, a couple of months before Angel was scheduled to graduate. It had been shortly after her funeral that he first began to talk about leaving town.

Stef glanced at the clock again and took a last bite of her sandwich. "Gotta go," she said. "Call me, okay? Are you going to see Angel again?"

Julie's smile was edged with bitterness. "Undoubtedly. This is a fairly small town, after all, and I'm sure I'll have the dubious pleasure of running into him."

Stef stood up and gave her friend's shoulder a squeeze. "Take care," she said, grabbing the check before Julie could protest. "I hope things work out however you want them to."

Julie said goodbye, but she had no hope that Stef's words would come true. How could they, when Julie didn't even know what she wanted?

An image flitted through her mind as she finished her iced tea, a picture of Angel begging her to take him back. In her imagination Julie was nonchalantly shaking her head and attempting to walk away as he threw himself at her feet in desperation, clinging to her ankles.

The mental picture brought a reluctant smile to her lips. It was almost the exact reverse of the way things really went. Then, she'd done and said all she could think of to keep him from leaving, and at one point she had been the one on her knees. That was before she'd ended up in his arms, so sure she had persuaded him to change his mind. What a stupid fool she'd been!

She wadded up her napkin and tossed it onto the table, vowing grimly never to let him know how much his departure had hurt her, or how strongly attracted she still was. He'd taken everything else she'd offered, but she'd be damned if she'd let him have the remnants of her pride.

"Julianna, telephone." Her mother's voice floated up the stairs.

Julie had left another message for Mrs. Hansen that morning. It had been three weeks since the dance, and

Julie hoped the call was about a permanent job some-where in the district. She was eager to get started and had specified that location wasn't important. She was willing to go upriver toward Concrete, or out to La Conner if she had to.

"Hello." Julie made no attempt to disguise the eagerness in her voice.

There was a moment's silence, and she suddenly felt a prickling sensation at the back of her neck. Even before he spoke she knew who was on the line.

"I'm glad I caught you at home." The words were simple, the voice arousing a complex of emotions Julie couldn't even begin to analyze.

"What do you want?" She gripped the receiver tighter and glanced around the empty hallway.

Again he hesitated, just long enough for Julie's mind to fill in a half dozen outrageous responses. Don't be a fool, she cautioned herself. He hasn't returned to Clarkson for *you*.

On the other end of the wire, Angel was wondering how to begin. He had thought of her often since their last meeting, but it seemed like his every waking minute had been filled with endless duties. He hadn't examined too closely the reasons he wanted her to head the adult literacy program at the center, but he knew deep inside that it was more than a business decision. He'd figured on settling for someone with the basic qualifications; finding a certified teacher to take the job would almost be too good to be true.

"I'd like to see you," he said carefully, "to discuss a possible position at the center."

It was Julie's turn to hesitate. His words had caught her totally by surprise. "What kind of position?"

"I would prefer to talk in person. Lunch today, if you're free."

After a brief struggle with the lump in her throat, she managed to match his cool, businesslike tone. If he wanted to ignore their last volatile exchange, she could, too. "Let me check my calendar." Covering the receiver with her hand, she counted to ten slowly, then added another five for good measure.

"I'm sorry, I have other plans." She made her voice sound politely regretful.

"Tomorrow?" he asked. Angel had a feeling she was playing with him, and he didn't like it one bit. He pictured the sophisticated beauty he'd seen at the country club, trying to reconcile her image with that of the pretty high school girl he'd left behind. The years had finally added the polish she had despaired of ever attaining, he thought grimly. Even when she'd been angry, hazel eyes deepened to fathomless green, she still attracted him.

She had mentioned that she didn't have a steady job, and perhaps she didn't really want one. Her parents were rich, and she was living with them. Had she changed that much? He remembered the Julie of long ago, her dreams and ambitions. Joining the ranks of the idle rich hadn't figured in them at all.

Something he didn't look at too closely drove him to keep pressing. "When's your first free day?" he asked when she didn't respond.

"Tomorrow would be fine." For a moment he heard her voice quiver before she leveled it out again. "Where shall we meet?"

"I could call for you." He'd never been to her parents' house, had only driven by it once with friends late at night. It was an imposing structure, white, with three stories and tall pillars in front. It was set back from the road like a family plantation, surrounded by a wrought iron fence designed to keep the likes of him out, and Julie in.

Julie felt a moment of panic. She wasn't ready to deal with him on her home ground, and she didn't want to make the explanations that his presence there would necessitate. "No. I could meet you at Sophia's at noon. Would that do?" Sophia's was a popular restaurant in Mount Vernon.

"Fine. Until tomorrow."

Angel hung up before she could change her mind. Ignoring the feeling of exultation that poured through him, he grabbed his keys and called to Joey, who was in the kitchen.

"I'll be out the rest of the day. See you at dinner."

Julie took a last sip of herb tea and carefully blotted her lips with her napkin. Angel was slouched in his chair, drinking his coffee and watching her through narrowed eyes. They'd managed to fill in the silent spaces during lunch with small talk about local growth, a marked change from the last time they had been face to face, but she had finally run out of conversation.

Julie resisted the urge to fidget as the silence between them lengthened. Setting down her cup, she prepared to wait as long as it took for Angel to introduce the reason for their meeting. She was curious about the job he'd mentioned over the phone but determined not to let her impatience show. The other questions that crowded her mind, she stubbornly ignored.

Angel reached toward his breast pocket, then let his hand drop. She wondered if he'd quit smoking recently. One of the newspaper photographs she'd se-

cretly clipped out several months before had shown him
with a cigarette in his mouth. Perhaps he was less relaxed than he wanted her to think.

"Would you like anything else?"

She shook her head. "No, thank you."

He took a last sip of his coffee and signaled the waitress for the check. Perhaps they weren't going to talk
about the center or a job opening after all. Maybe he'd
only used that as an excuse, but why?

The whole lunch had been an exercise in impersonal
politeness, except for the occasional flash of indeci-
pherable emotion she'd seen in Angel's eyes when a location or person linked to their shared past was
mentioned inadvertently.

Julie was glad she'd worn one of her new, flattering
outfits. After careful consideration that morning, she'd
settled on a sage-green linen dress topped by a green-
and-peach plaid blazer. It might be a little fancy for
lunch, but the green made her hazel eyes appear brighter, and flattered the brown of her hair. She'd spent
longer than usual at her vanity table, thinking all the
while about canceling altogether. Curiosity, and the
desire to see Angel again, had kept her from picking up
the phone. If his detached attitude toward her during
lunch was a disappointment, his appearance almost
made up for it.

He was wearing a charcoal-gray suit, and hers hadn't
been the only head that had turned when he walked into
the restaurant. His lean build and broad shoulders along
with his shining raven hair and his eyes a shade darker
than the blue silk of his tie, attracted the attention of
every woman in the room.

"That's the race car driver who was in that magazine a few months ago," a white-haired woman at the

next table had exclaimed to her companion as Angel spoke to the hostess. "He could put his slippers under my bed anytime he chose."

The woman with her had cackled in response. "He'd stall your pacemaker."

If Julie hadn't been so tense, she would have grinned at the two old ladies. As it was, her cheeks had gone hot when he had strolled across the room to where she sat, pausing before pulling out a chair.

"You look beautiful," he had said. It was the last personal remark he made.

Now Julie schooled her expression and tried to quell the little tremors that ran through her as she returned his brooding gaze with a steady one of her own.

"If you have the time, there's someplace I'd like to show you," Angel said, a brief smile lighting his face, then disappearing as abruptly as it came. "The building for the center is only a short drive from here."

"Perhaps you should tell me about the position you mentioned first," she said. "I might not be interested, and then this excursion would be pointless."

Angel sighed and shifted in his chair. "All right. We discussed adult literacy the other evening and you mentioned that you're a teacher. It's one of the first programs I want to get started at the center, and I want you to organize it."

Julie's eyes widened. "Me?"

"Why not?"

She thought for a moment. "How do you know if I'm suitable? Surely there's someone more—"

He leaned forward. "Let me list your qualifications," he said, interrupting. He held up one hand, ticking off each point. "You're unemployed, eager and, hopefully, you'll work cheap. You have a teaching de-

gree. There's a short course on the newest methods that
you can take, down in Everett, and I have a stack of lit-
erature you can go through.''

Julie was still trying to keep back a smile at his reasoning. ''What makes you think I'll work cheap?'' she
asked.

''Because you need a job,'' he shot back. ''And because of what I'm going to show you.'' Suddenly his
face lit up. ''There's such a need for this whole project,'' he said, voice low and passionate. ''I visited several places like it in California, and I know we could do
something similar, even better, here. We have a large
population of Chicanos who desperately need this kind
of facility.''

He reached across the table to grip Julie's hand in his.
She was sure he hadn't even realized what he was doing,
but her nerves began to dance with excitement from the
warmth of his touch.

''You would be in charge of tutors, applications,
matching people together and helping them if they ran
into problems. I know you could do it.'' His eyes were
sparkling, and his brooding expression had been trans-
formed. Julie found herself caught up in his enthusiasm.

''I've taught reading to children,'' she said. ''There's
something so uplifting about sharing that knowledge
and opening the world of books to someone else.'' She
wasn't quite ready to confess that she'd already taken
the specialized training he'd mentioned, and that she'd
had a year of high school Spanish after he'd left town.

His expression softened at her words, bringing sudden moisture to her eyes. ''I knew you'd understand,''
he said as she blinked to hide her reaction. ''Think
about opening up that world to an adult who's always

been shut out. Bringing the skills to many adults who, until now, never thought they'd be part of that world.''

Angel gazed at her for a long moment, picturing her working alongside him, making his dream come true. It was more than he had hoped for; perhaps he was being foolish. Julie's fingers squeezed his, and he stared at their linked hands before jerking away as if he'd been burned.

Good lord, working together was undoubtedly a terrible idea.

"Are you interested?" he asked gruffly, avoiding her eyes.

"Yes," Julie replied, surprising him. "I think I am."

"We'd better discuss salary," he said and named a modest amount. "Until you have the reading program running, you'd be working in other areas, too, as the need arises. There will be plenty of work."

"Other areas?" She wondered where the money for her salary was coming from. Probably Angel's own pocket.

"Wait until you see the building. It's been unoccupied for quite a while. After we have it cleaned out, we'll have to set up the offices and everything else."

Angel shoved out his chair, then grasped the back of hers. "I was only kidding about your helping with the cleaning, but there will be plenty to keep you busy. Still interested?"

She nodded, not bothering to comment on his apparent assumption that she thought she was too good to help with the scrub work. He'd find out soon enough that if she took the job, she would have no qualms about getting her hands dirty. Meanwhile, if he wanted to think of her as a helpless socialite, that was his problem.

"Come on, then," he said. "Let's go for a ride."

While he paid the check, Julie tried to sort out the emotions that had tumbled through her the past hour. Angel was as complex as an unsolvable math equation. He'd changed from distant businessman to enthusiastic idealist, while she'd been trying to keep her own response to him under control.

Each expression of his handsome face brought back memories. He had inherited his straight nose and high cheekbones from his mother. Julie had only met her once, but she remembered the woman's Castilian beauty, despite her age and hard life.

Angel's voice when he spoke over his shoulder aroused feelings in Julie she couldn't control, and his eyes...his eyes invited her to let down her guard and release the emotions that clamored to get out. She rubbed her forehead slowly as she followed him to the gleaming black Ferrari.

"Headache?" he asked solicitously, opening the passenger door.

"No. I was just thinking how persuasive you can be." Their eyes met for a timeless moment, Julie remembering too late the last time she'd spoken almost exactly the same words. It had been when Angel finally convinced her to run away with him.

Anger seeped into his face. It was obvious that he remembered, too. "Get in." His voice had turned to cold steel.

She hesitated, then chided herself as she slid onto the leather seat. Fear had no place in her relationship with Angel, not then and not now. She might be wary of her own reactions to his presence, but he would never hurt her. At least not physically. Unlike some men who abused women to feel like real men, Angel's manhood had never been in doubt.

He drove very fast but skillfully toward the west side of town.

"Is this how you won races?" she couldn't resist asking as he slammed the brakes hard to avoid a car that had turned in front of him.

"What? Oh, sorry." His sudden grin made her breath catch in her throat. He'd always been quick to anger and equally quick to cool. "Everyone drives like this in California. I guess I'd better be careful or I'll get a ticket. I heard that Rudy Juarez is on the police force now."

She nodded. "I've seen him in his patrol car." She was going to ask about some of the other people from high school, but he braked again and turned a corner onto a narrow gravel road she'd never been down before, moving toward some old buildings.

Julie wondered what her parents would think about this job if she took it. The position was a far cry from volunteer tutoring at the community college. Then she chided herself. She was past the age of always considering how her parents would react.

Angel pulled up before an empty two-story building and turned off the engine. "Welcome to *Casa del Sol,* the House of the Sun," he said, looking at her. "Want to go inside?"

"Sure." She looked around dubiously. Plenty of parking, but the building was fairly close to the older, less affluent part of town. She got out of the car, following him up the front steps.

Angel pulled out a key and unlocked the door. First he showed her the main floor—two offices with a smaller connecting room in between, then several bigger rooms including a kitchen.

"My office," he said, indicating a room already furnished with a scarred desk, a phone and a lamp, a chair and a battered file cabinet. On every available surface were piles of neatly stacked papers and folders. A note pad was covered with lists, some of the items crossed off.

"You've been busy," Julie commented.

"I've only scratched the surface of what needs to be done."

"Have you been working alone?"

He leaned against the doorjamb, crossing his arms. Julie took a step back, and his eyes sparked.

"You wouldn't believe the help I've had, and the offers of labor, donated items, even food. A group of women from the community has been coming every day to clean. Some of the men have been painting, and they've hauled several loads of trash out of here."

Julie noticed that the office walls had been recently covered in a warm, ivory tone that made the room appear larger.

"Word is getting around, and people are responding," he continued. "One thing I'd hoped to set up is a schedule of available workers, so we don't have ten men standing around idle one day and no one here the next."

Julie was amazed at what he'd already accomplished, and said so. She couldn't sort through what she felt, seeing this dream of his and having the chance to participate in it. Why had he chosen to quit racing and do this? Some people said the terrible collision that had killed one of the other top drivers had taken away Angel's nerve. He hadn't bothered to publicly deny the speculative stories that appeared on the sports pages when he quit. Julie would have liked to ask him about it, but their relationship, if they had one, was going to be strictly business, and she'd do well to remember that.

"Come on," he said after a moment. "I don't want the upstairs to shock you. We haven't done much there yet."

As they walked through an adjoining room, he explained that it would serve for a secretary when he found one. A young Chicano woman whose husband had been killed in a field accident looked like a good possibility, especially if they opened the day-care center Angel hoped for. The woman had small children.

They paused in another doorway. "Your office, if you take the job." There was an old, gray metal desk, a chair and a file cabinet, one empty drawer hanging open. The walls had been painted a pale blue, and the brown linoleum floor was scarred but clean and freshly waxed. Julie could already picture the room with a plant on the desk, perhaps a couple of colorful posters and a big calendar on the walls.

"This building's in pretty good shape," she commented when they looked at the kitchen. "What did it used to be?"

"Some kind of freight business. There's a loading dock off the other end."

"How did you—?"

"Actually, your father donated the building. It was sitting empty."

Julie's mouth gaped open. So she hadn't known, Angel thought.

"Why would he do that? Mother's done volunteer work for years, but I've never known Dad to take any interest in charitable causes. He's too wrapped up in his company."

"Why don't you ask him?"

"I'm asking you." She looked as if she wasn't going to budge until he answered.

Angel thought a moment before speaking. "He said it was for tax purposes, but I got the impression that he wants to do something for the people who work for him, and for their families. Your father's an interesting man. We had quite a talk, and he asked a lot of questions about my plans." Angel remembered that John Remington had raised some points Angel hadn't considered. "The office furniture is from him, too."

Julie considered the information he'd just given her. "Perhaps I've misjudged him," she murmured.

"Perhaps you have. Let's go upstairs." Angel moved down the hallway. "There are two rest rooms in working order, through there."

The second floor was divided into two huge rooms. There was a pile of cardboard cartons and broken furniture in one corner, and the walls all needed paint badly. Some of the floor tiles were torn and peeling.

"Plenty of room for the kids," Angel said proudly. "With a bathroom and classroom space."

He knew the building was almost perfect for what he wanted. When John Remington had showed it to him, he had thought it would be expensive. Instead he was getting the use of it for nothing.

Julie started back toward the stairs, and he followed her.

"What's in this room?" she asked, opening a door in the hallway. It was only a supply closet. She stopped abruptly and turned, moving right into Angel's waiting arms.

For a timeless moment they both froze, so close their bodies were almost touching, his fingers framing her face, her hands raised as if to ward him off.

He made no move to step back as she stared into his eyes. The blue flames in their depths leaped higher. Julie's heart began tripping erratically, and her breath caught. She could smell his Dark Angel cologne, deep and musky. He didn't appear to be breathing.

Slowly his hand caressed her cheek. Her chin rose automatically as she looked at his full lips, remembering their warmth, their flavor, with an aching, spreading need.

"Haven't you wondered," he whispered huskily, "how it would be?" His thumb flicked across her mouth, and a tremor rippled through Julie. "Would the kiss be as sweet now as it was when we loved?" He bent closer. "Aren't you curious, Julie?"

His words penetrated, the pain stabbing her like a thousand shards of ice. It was only an experiment he wanted. She waited stiffly as he came closer, his shoulders blotting out the dim light.

Angel's fingers tightened along the sides of her face. "You've had lovers," he murmured, "and a husband. I've changed, too. Shall we compare what we've learned?" His breath fanned her hair as his words broke her heart.

When his mouth touched hers, she flowed against him helplessly for a moment, his familiar warmth seeping into her, his lips on hers the sweetest of sensations. Then realizing what she was allowing to happen, she pushed him away furiously.

She blazed up at him, "Don't you touch me again! I was crazy to consider working for you, and I don't want to compare techniques!'' Her lips tingled, and the breath heaved in her chest. ''Take me back to my car.''

Without looking to see if he followed, she clattered down the stairs and out the double front door.

Angel came after her slowly, hands jammed deep into his pockets as he tried to slow the slamming of his heart and quell the fiery urges of his body. What the hell had come over him, acting the way he had? She would never help him if she thought he was going to make passes every time they were alone. And what had possessed him to say those things?

Had he been trying to hide his own vulnerability in wanting to kiss her? Of course he had. Her nearness had inflamed him, and he had acted instinctively, covering up his feelings with that insane drivel about comparisons.

He banged the front door closed, relieved to see that Julie was waiting in the car. His hands shook as he slowly turned the key in its lock, and he searched for the right words of apology before he went to face her. The only thing he was really sorry about was that he hadn't kissed her properly when he had the chance.

Chapter Four

Julie watched Angel lock the front door of the center and walk to where she sat huddled in the car, seething with reaction. His face was impassive—brilliant eyes shuttered and mouth drawn into a grim line. When he climbed in beside her she didn't turn. Instead she stared straight ahead through the windshield. Seconds ticked by as the strain between them mounted.

"I blew it, didn't I?"

The bluntness of his question surprised her, and she didn't respond immediately, still hurt at the way he'd insulted the love they'd once shared.

"I'm sorry, it was a stupid move."

He reached out to her and she swiveled to face him, shrinking against the passenger door before she could stop herself. Something blazed in his eyes and he jerked back, raking his hand through his straight dark hair before he doubled it into a fist and thumped the steering wheel.

"Don't let what happened between us stop you from taking this job."

Julie wasn't sure if he was referring to what they had once meant to each other or his kiss moments before, but apparently all he was concerned about now was his precious center. That hurt.

"You can do a lot of good here, and I promise that—" Angel gestured toward the building "—won't happen again." He wrapped both hands around the steering wheel, ducking his head as he stretched his arms and flexed his powerful shoulders. "It's no excuse, but I guess I'm too tired to have good sense right now. I've been putting in some long hours."

Julie didn't know what to say. If she had any common sense of her own, she would still be waiting for a teaching position at one of the area schools, instead of sitting here in Angel's Ferrari while he assured her that he'd only kissed her because he was too tired to know better!

She opened her mouth to tell him she had changed her mind, that the whole idea was a mistake, but before she could speak, he interrupted again, frowning darkly.

"I need you here," he almost growled, as if the words were being pulled from him. "You'd be perfect for the job and you know it, and I don't have time to find someone else."

Julie almost laughed. She couldn't remember ever having been given a less flattering reason to do something. If she hadn't already decided that she could make a real difference, she would refuse him immediately. Instead she stared, while he took a turn gazing straight ahead. Only the whiteness of his knuckles on the wheel betrayed his tension.

"I don't know," she said slowly. "I need to think."

Angel remained silent. Apparently he'd said all he was going to on the subject. He made no move to start the engine, and she shifted restlessly. The job was perfect for her, and if he could shove personal feelings aside, so could she. Then she reminded herself that he didn't have personal feelings where she was concerned anymore. If she refused the offer, he might think it was because she did.

Julie squared her shoulders and cast her reservations to the wind. It was about time she took a few chances. Immediately she remembered the last momentous decision she'd made, while still full of doubts—marrying Brad. Could this decision result in anything more disastrous? Still, seeing Angel every day would only be a complication if she allowed it to be. No job was perfect.

"I accept your offer."

If she had expected some big reaction from Angel, she was disappointed. He let out his breath and reached for the ignition key.

"Good," was all he said, and he didn't even look at her as he backed up and headed toward the restaurant where she'd left her car. After a moment he brought up the tutoring course in Everett he wanted her to take.

Julie had to suppress a smile. "That won't be necessary."

He glanced at her, annoyed, as he began to argue. "I really think you need it."

"No."

"Don't be stubborn. It isn't that tough."

He was beginning to show signs of temper, and she decided that she'd strung him along enough. "I know how tough the course is. I've already taken it. *And* I'm certified."

The car swerved alarmingly.

"You are? Why didn't you tell me when I mentioned it before?"

For a moment Julie glimpsed some of the old interest, the old spark on Angel's face, before he quickly schooled his features into indifference.

She shrugged. "I have to have a few secrets."

He ignored her comment. "Well," he said, pleased, "that will save some time."

She expected to hear from him again soon, but it was almost a week before they spoke. Apparently he'd been serious about her not doing any cleaning up; when he did call, Julie had to argue before he agreed that she could come in to help the next Saturday morning. On Friday, as she finished up her last day of substitute teaching, she found herself looking forward to her next visit to the center with a lot more enthusiasm than a floor-scrubbing session warranted.

"Miss Remington, can I clean the blackboard?"

Julie smiled down at the eager little boy who stood shifting his weight from one foot to the other. "That would be very nice, Jimmy. Thank you."

Julie had been filling in at a grade school in Mount Vernon all week, and she would miss the children she had been teaching. With a sigh, she cleared off her desk, marveling at how rapidly the room had emptied.

Jimmy finished the blackboard and took the erasers outside to clean. After the door shut behind him, Julie stood and walked to the window. She shoved her hands deep into the patch pockets of her full skirt and thought about Angel.

The memory of his voice on the phone the evening before made her insides flutter. He was always so excited when he talked about the center, so full of passion. He'd felt that way about her once, but that had been a long time ago. Common sense told her to be glad those feelings were dead, but common sense didn't have anything to do with Julie's feelings for Angel. She told herself it was only memories that made her so aware of him physically. Memories and the virile handsomeness that must have earned him a fortune in product endorsements.

The door swung open. "I'm done, Miss Remington," Jimmy said, putting down the erasers before he grabbed his lunch box and coat.

"Thanks for your help." She smiled at him as he struggled to do up his buttons.

"Will Mrs. Eliason be back on Monday?"

"Yes, she will." Mrs. Eliason was the teacher Julie had been substituting for.

"Good. Well, bye." Jimmy raced out the door, letting it bang shut behind him.

"Bye." Julie began putting her things into the large tote bag she used for teaching. She'd already told Mrs. Hansen about her new job and asked to be removed from the substitute teaching list. Burned her bridges, her mother would have said.

Leaving a note clipped to Mrs. Eliason's lesson plan, Julie took a last look around the room before stepping into the hallway. Her life was taking another drastic turn, and she wasn't entirely convinced it was for the better. In some ways the new job at the center was a dream, but if she didn't keep her attraction to Angel under tight control, it could prove to be a nightmare. Remembering his offhand kiss didn't help.

Julie stopped at the front desk of the school to fill out some papers and say goodbye to the office staff.

"We'll probably be seeing you again," the secretary said.

"Not for a while. I've accepted a full-time job at the new Chicano center."

"Doing what?"

"Setting up the adult literacy program." Julie couldn't keep the pride from entering her voice at being part of something so worthwhile.

One of the aides stopped sorting papers. "I think that's terrific. We've needed something like that for a long time. When's the center going to open?"

"Soon, but I'm not exactly sure just when," Julie replied, taking a last look around the lobby. "All I know is that I'm spending tomorrow washing floors and painting walls."

The secretary frowned. "I thought you said—"

Julie's chuckle stopped her. "I know what I said, but everyone down there has been pitching in to get the place ready. You wouldn't believe the number of volunteers we've had. I've been here teaching all week, but tomorrow I start doing my share."

Saying goodbye, Julie pushed her way out the front door, dodged two boys who weren't supposed to be riding bikes on the sidewalk and headed for her car. She had enjoyed the week with the children, but was eager to start the next phase of her life.

From what Angel had said when he'd called, the office supplies had come in, her telephone was installed and the receptionist he'd hired already had a tentative list of people who had made inquiries about the reading program.

Julie's responsibilities would include putting the prospective tutors through a brief, intensive training course, then pairing each with a student on a one-to-one basis. She would be available if any problems arose, and hoped to do some individual tutoring of her own, but Angel had made it clear there would be plenty of other work to keep her busy. The adult literacy program was only one small item on the list of services he intended to offer eventually.

Julie turned her car onto the highway and headed toward her parents' home. Slowing to make the turn through the wrought iron gates of the country club, she waved at two of her father's friends who were pulling their golf carts across the road. She hadn't told her mother or father about the new job yet, planning on doing that at dinner that evening. Afterward, her parents were going to a dance that Julie's mother had tried to get her to attend with them.

Now that her high school crowd had grown up and intermarried, Julie found that she had even less in common with them than before, though she had been readily accepted into their circle when she had married Brad. A busy social life was important to him, and she had tried to fit in, but after their separation she was relieved to drift out of the group again.

A couple of people had expressed sympathy when she and Brad split up; one of the husbands had even offered to console her. The knowledge that her personal life was being gossiped about was difficult to take, and Julie was actually relieved when Suzy Martin grabbed the spotlight by getting caught naked in her hot tub with the gardener. Julie found the endless speculations over who was doing what with whom exceedingly tiresome, and it was easy to turn down this invitation of her parents'.

Maybe she'd give Stef a call. If her friend didn't already have plans, they could see a movie together. Julie needed some lightweight entertainment after the week she'd put in, and it would help speed the time until Saturday.

The next morning Julie was already seated at the breakfast table when Mrs. Remington walked in. "You're up early," she said, smiling.

Julie paused before biting into her croissant. "Stef wasn't home last night, so I didn't stay up very late. Besides, I have to be at the center at eight. How was the dance?"

To her surprise, when she had told her parents about the new job, neither had expressed any negative feelings. Her father had been particularly supportive. Perhaps they were just relieved she was showing an interest in something, but if they had known about her prior history with Angel they would feel differently, she was sure.

Now Julie's mother slid into a chair across the table and poured coffee from the silver carafe. "The dance was fine, same crowd as always. The Fergusons are just back from their cruise, and the McKays are leaving for Scottsdale in the morning." She sipped her coffee. "Oh, that nice Michael Christian asked for you."

Julie hastily blotted her lips with her napkin, hiding a wry smile. It had probably been the other way around, knowing her mother and her firm belief that a woman needed a man in attendance to feel complete. She had probably mentioned Julie to Michael.

"I thought he was married?"

"Divorced. And becoming very successful with his real estate business." Mrs. Remington smiled innocently.

Julie glanced at her watch and drained her coffee cup. "I'm happy for Michael, but I have to run or I'll be late. Don't know when I'll be home, so don't worry about dinner."

"Did you forget, dear? We're going to the Ferguson's. No doubt they'll have slides of the cruise. I'll tell Ginny to leave you something." Ginny was the housekeeper.

Julie ran her hands along the faded jeans she was wearing. She had on an equally shabby sweatshirt, its sleeves hacked off at the elbows. No point in dressing up to scrub floors. "Don't bother Ginny. I can put something in the microwave."

"As long as you eat," her mother was saying as Julie called goodbye and dashed out the front door. Sometimes Julie was still treated as if she were ten. Now that she had a steady job it was time to look for a place of her own, but she wouldn't be able to afford anything fancy on the salary Angel was paying her. She wouldn't need much; a small apartment that was easy to take care of would be ideal. She'd never been on her own, what with college and then marriage to Brad, and she found herself looking forward to the idea of being truly independent for the first time in her life. It would be fun, and it was certainly long overdue.

When Julie pulled up at the center, there were several cars and pickups parked in front, all of them older models, but Angel's gleaming Ferrari wasn't among them. Ignoring the little dive her stomach took, Julie took a deep breath and went inside.

She heard a woman's voice coming from the direction of the offices, chattering in rapid Spanish. Julie, whose year of high school Spanish was getting rusty, could barely pick out a word here and there. Footsteps creaked overhead, so someone was already working upstairs where they'd be painting today. Julie had just turned toward the stairway when she heard Angel's deep voice coming from down the hall.

"Connie, you know I don't speak Spanish. Now say that again. In English, if you please." His voice sounded light, teasing, and it brought back a flood of memories. Julie turned her steps toward his office.

Connie was the receptionist he'd hired. She had three little children, and her husband had been killed the summer before when a tractor overturned on him. Julie hadn't met her yet, but Angel had been impressed with Connie's determination in taking secretarial courses at night. Listening to him sing her praises, Julie had told herself disgruntledly that she ought to be glad he'd found such a paragon.

"There you are," he said when she walked through the open doorway. His gaze slid down her body and back up again before he gave her a grin. "And dressed to work, I see."

She didn't know quite how to take that, and had to bite back the retort that sprang to the tip of her tongue. Had he really thought she wasn't serious about helping? His own lean frame was covered with a black T-shirt that hugged his broad shoulders, and bleached jeans with a hole in one knee. They were tight, the fabric clinging to his lean hips and muscular thighs. Julie found herself mesmerized by the big, silver belt buckle that rode low on his waist.

"This is Connie Ramirez," Angel said, breaking the silence. "Julianna Remington."

"Julie," she corrected, smiling at a petite woman with long black hair and big brown eyes.

Connie returned her smile. "Don't let his teasing bother you," she said. "We need all the able bodies we can get to strip that floor upstairs." Her words, meant to be friendly, only succeeded in making Julie feel like an outsider. She'd dealt with more of Angel's teasing than Connie ever would, Julie thought resentfully. Then realizing the path her thoughts were taking, she pulled up short. "So where are the buckets?" she asked.

By the time they broke for lunch, sweat was trickling between her breasts and down the side of her neck, but the old linoleum in one big room was finally freed of its layers of yellowed wax. Julie, Connie and two men named Juan and Ben had worked together.

Angel was downstairs replacing some of the pipes under the kitchen and bathroom sinks. Several times that morning they had heard a loud metallic crash followed by a shouted curse, causing Julie and Connie to exchange amused grins. Now, wiping her forehead with an old handkerchief, Julie was glad Angel hadn't been on the second floor with them as she got steadily dirtier and more disheveled.

Footsteps thundered up the wooden staircase as she slowly straightened the protesting muscles in her back.

"All done?" Angel asked. "I'm going to make a lunch run. Who wants what?"

He wrote down everyone's orders, then looked directly at Julie. "Want to come and help me carry everything?"

His offer surprised her. "I have to make a phone call—" she began, remembering the apartment for rent she'd been told to check back on at noon. The place sounded promising, and it was fairly close to the center.

He shrugged. "Okay. Connie?"

Julie had hoped he would wait for her, but the other woman smiled and agreed to go before Julie could react. She followed them downstairs as Connie chattered happily about how wonderful the day-care center was going to be when they got everything set up. Angel was listening attentively as he held open the front door for her, and Julie went to call about the apartment with considerably less enthusiasm than she'd had all morning.

Angel shifted the bags of food so he could pull the door back open for Connie, who was carrying the containers of soft drinks. Connie was nice, and pretty in a dark, seductive way. Her bubbly, easygoing personality had come as a shock to Angel after her flirtatious eyes and sexy build. She looked like a vamp, and acted like a kid sister. The grief she'd felt, and the struggle she'd been through after her husband's death, were well hidden beneath her warm smile and friendly personality. He liked her, but he still wished Julie hadn't refused his offer. He'd only turned to Connie to cover his disappointment. Nice as she was, her incessant chatter could drive him crazy in a short length of time.

"Chow's here," he shouted as they entered the building and headed for the kitchen where there was a long table and some folding chairs.

The others were already there, sitting around discussing the things they wanted the center to have.

"Job placement," said Ben, crushing his cigarette into a pottery ashtray.

"Vocational training." Juan worked in the fields during the summer, and his family went on welfare in the off-season while he tried to find odd jobs.

"A good day-care center," Connie said, passing out the drinks.

Angel set down the bags of food. "All that and more," he said. "God willing, plus enough donations, and volunteers to help with the work."

Julie had been washing up at the big kitchen sink, not letting herself turn around the minute she heard Angel's voice. Now she took a chair between Connie and Juan and began to eat her warm taco.

"What about you," Angel asked, his blue eyes meeting hers. "What else do you want to see?"

Caught by surprise, Julie hesitated, chewing thoughtfully. She tried to ignore the tightness in her chest that Angel's attention instantly produced.

"Programs for teens," she said after a moment. "Somewhere for them to hang out, some counseling so they won't drop out of school like so many did—" She stopped abruptly, realizing she'd been thinking back to when she and Angel had been in high school. A strong instinct told her to avoid mentioning it. "Like so many do," she corrected, gaze dropping to the taco shell she'd crushed between her fingers.

"Good idea," Angel said, filling the puzzled silence. He knew the others were curious about the tension between him and Julie. None of them had been in school with the two of them, but undoubtedly word would get around soon enough. He hadn't yet decided how he'd handle the questions when they came. Part of him wanted to forget those days, but another part, the part that responded every time he looked at Julie, still wanted the truth. Why had she changed her mind?

"I have to go," Connie said, crumpling up the wrappers from her lunch. "Mama is watching my kids, but I told her I'd be back by one."

"Thanks for coming in," Angel said. "I'll see you on Monday, and we'll make the day-care center a prime priority. I hope that in one more week you'll be bringing your children here with you."

Connie smiled. "That would be wonderful. I'm glad all the permits have come through. The place where I've been leaving my kids during the week is dirty, and the woman doesn't pay much attention to them, but it's all I could find."

She said goodbye and left.

"Connie's right," Juan said. "Some of the places we leave our children are real holes, but who can afford better?"

"Soon it will be different," Angel told him. "Now let's get that other room upstairs painted."

He and Julie worked side by side all afternoon, but neither spoke, except to comment on the job they were doing. She painted the trim around the windows with white enamel, while the men rolled the walls with pale yellow, washable latex. More than once Julie stepped back as if to check her work, but in truth she was watching the smooth way Angel's muscles moved as he stretched and bent with the roller.

The afternoon grew steadily warmer. Finally Angel stopped, mopping his brow with a dark blue bandanna. Julie turned to ask him something, but the words stuck in her throat as he yanked the dark T-shirt over his head.

Her mouth went dry as his bare, broad chest was revealed, a round medal on a silver chain gleaming against his honeyed skin. While she stared helplessly, paintbrush dripping white enamel, Angel freed his head and tossed the shirt aside. He noticed Julie, and for a long moment their eyes met and held. Then his gaze dropped.

"Good thing those are old shoes."

"What?" Julie followed the direction of his gaze to the drips of white paint. "Oh!" She reached for the rag and bent down, face flooding with heat.

She was glad that the other two men were busy arguing about who was going to finish the brushwork along the ceiling and hadn't noticed her exchange with Angel. It was bad enough that Angel himself had seen her struggle for control.

Straightening, Julie ignored the stare she could almost feel and dipped her brush in the paint can, trying to focus her complete attention on the molding before her.

Muttering a curse under his breath, Angel turned and began to roll paint on the wall with such force that the roller spattered him. Swearing again, he wiped his face with the bandanna.

Julie was lost in a sea of memories as she carefully worked on the wood trim. The sight of Angel barechested had brought back with aching clarity another scene, one that was etched into her heart.

Back in school she'd loved Angel with an innocence that he tried hard not to shatter when they were together. He never kissed her as long or as often as she would have liked, always pulling away just when she thought he was going to really kiss her like a man kissed a woman. At the time he'd answered her questions with joking replies, lighting a cigarette and taking deep drags, his hands shaking. Or he would get out of her car and walk around for a few minutes before rejoining her.

His actions had puzzled her until that one afternoon, an unseasonably hot day, when she had met him at their private spot along the river.

Julie had been early, but Angel was already there. She'd parked on the dirt road and walked through the tall grass down to the riverbank. It was obvious that Angel had been swimming; water dripped from his hair and beaded on his deeply tanned skin as he bent to zip the jeans he'd just pulled on.

Hearing her approach, he straightened abruptly. Julie had been too busy staring at the muscles that rippled across his shoulders and down his chest to notice his expression. The water clung to him in droplets, trickling down his flat abdomen and disappearing into the low waistband of his worn jeans.

Watching her silently, Angel dropped his hands away from the snap and approached her slowly.

"You're early."

Julie could barely detect the strain in his voice over the roaring noise that filled her ears. She went up to him, raising her hands and placing them on his shoulders, feeling the coolness of his chilled skin. Wonder gripped her as she felt the warmth seep back into him, then flow to her. Angel trembled beneath her touch.

"Cold?" she asked, finding her voice.

His arm came around her. "No, baby. Not cold." Angel bent his head, and Julie raised hers to meet his descending mouth. With the kiss they shared, she became suddenly, achingly aware of what passion meant. This time when Angel pulled away to take a cigarette from the pack on the ground and light it with shaking hands, she didn't complain. Instead she shocked him by asking that he light one for her, too.

He'd refused. "I've already taught you too much," he said. "I'll be damned if I teach you how to smoke, too."

"You done with this window?"

Julie blinked at Ben, wondering what on earth he was talking about. Then she came back to the present with a crash, glancing hastily at Angel to see if he'd noticed her temporary absence. He hadn't; he was still busy with the wall.

"Yes. I'll do the trim around the door now." She forced a smile and picked up the paint can, not looking at Ben.

Angel dimly heard the exchange, but he was too busy with his own thoughts for it to make much of an impression. If Julie looked at him like that again, he was very likely to embarrass both of them. When it came to her, he was beginning to realize he had no more control than he'd had as a hot-blooded teenager. No woman had aroused him as Julie did, and no encounter had been as sweet as the one he remembered as clearly as if it had happened a month before.

Just thinking along those lines made Angel's body react in a distinctly uncomfortable manner. He set the roller down in the pan. "I have to run an errand," he announced to no one in particular, wiping his hands as he crossed the room in long strides. At the doorway he turned back, and his gaze met Julie's.

He frowned, making her wonder what had set him off. She listened to his boots clattering down the wooden steps, followed by the sound of the front door slamming.

"What's gotten into him?" Juan asked as they heard an engine roaring to life.

Ben shrugged, then went back to his painting. "He'll blow Joey's truck up if he keeps driving like that," he replied.

Julie knew that Joey was staying at Angel's new house, but she hadn't talked to him in years. She'd given in to the temptation to drive by there once, when she was reasonably sure that Angel wouldn't be home. She'd been impressed by the house. It was more modern than a lot of the residences in its exclusive neighborhood, but it blended in very nicely. The front was a mixture of brick and stained cedar siding, the roof dark brown tile.

She would have liked to slow down and really look, but was afraid Joey might see her cruising the cul-de-sac and mention it to Angel. That was the last thing she needed, for him to think she had anything but a professional interest in him. Now she wondered, as she scraped her paintbrush against the rim of the can, if he'd noticed the strength of her reaction when he peeled off his shirt. She didn't see how he could have missed it, but she hoped that somehow he had.

He hadn't returned when the three of them finished the room and took the equipment downstairs to clean it up.

Julie glanced at her watch. "Why don't you two go? I can finish here."

Juan and Ben exchanged glances. They'd been talking earlier about their plans for that night's entertainment, and she knew they would be eager to get going. Julie almost envied them.

"We can't leave you here alone," Juan finally said. "It wouldn't be a good idea."

The front door slammed, and Julie began to wish she hadn't volunteered.

"Angel must be back. Now we can go," Ben said, glancing at Julie. "You really don't mind?"

Angel walked into the room, and Julie could almost feel his gaze. "No, go ahead. It won't take me much time to clean the stuff you used. The latex paint will wash right off."

"Give me the brush you used on the enamel, and I'll take care of it," Angel said after the others left. He didn't even look at Julie as he took it from her, but there was a black expression on his face, and he moved stiffly, almost as if he was very tense about something. He took the brush and a can of turpentine outside as Julie cleaned up everything else in the big sink. The rollers' covers took quite a while, and she was still washing them, wishing she could just throw them away, when he returned.

"Where did you go earlier?" she asked without thinking as she glanced up.

Angel stared at her for a long moment. She decided he didn't intend to answer, but then he finally spoke. "I went down to the river. You probably don't remember the spot, but I wanted to see if it was still there. It's a good place to swim when the water's warm enough."

Julie swallowed. "I haven't been there for years. Did you swim?"

"Not today. I had a lot of thinking to do." After another silence, while Julie memorized the lean planes of his face, his straight nose and full lips, she forced herself to turn away.

"The upstairs is done if you want to check it," she said, giving the last roller a final squeeze.

"Yeah, I'll do that before I lock up. Why don't you go on home, you've put in a long day."

It was clear from the rigid set to his shoulders and the straight line of his black brows that he didn't want her there.

"Good idea," she said. "As soon as I wash my hands."

Without waiting, Angel went into his office, pushing the door shut after him.

Julie didn't bother to wish him good-night. She just picked up her purse and left.

The next week was a hectic one. The two women who'd been hired to run the day-care operation were in and out, having a ball buying games and supplies for the children. They were both young mothers themselves, and Julie found herself included in their conversations with Connie as if she were one of them. Before the week was over, she felt as if she really was. She often took time away from her own duties to watch their five children if they both had to run to the store for more supplies. She read some of the new picture books, fed the baby and helped the others put together some of the new puzzles. The oldest boy, Ronnie, was four, and he told Julie several times how eager he was to start school the next year.

Angel sometimes found himself forgetting all about the endless paperwork as he sat back in his chair and listened to the lighthearted conversation between Connie and Julie, whose office opened up from the other side of Connie's. Julie's ability to fit in had come as a surprise to him. For a long time he'd blamed her sudden defection on his background and his mixed blood, but it was obvious that she held no prejudices against the Mexicans at the center. She treated them all with warmth and respect, from the people who came to volunteer their time, to the migrant workers who stopped in looking for help.

Julie's attitude had Angel confused, and he didn't like it one bit. Before he could waste more time thinking about it, the center was ready for its official opening, and they were all busy planning the fiesta to celebrate the event. It was scheduled for the next Saturday, with an open house, games for the children and a big potluck dinner, followed by dancing for the adults who cared to stay.

Julie found herself in charge of decorations, and she had asked the advice of several of her new friends before deciding on colored lights, streamers, balloons and lots of crepe paper. Juan's wife was making up several piñatas for the children, and Ben's wife's cousin was organizing games and prizes. Connie's sister was in charge of the food. She and her husband owned a small restaurant and would furnish the basic menu. Volunteers would provide salads and desserts, and Angel was laying in an ample supply of soft drinks and Mexican beer that had been donated by a local distributor.

Given the network of relatives throughout the Hispanic community everyone seemed to possess, it was sad that Angel had no family other than Luis, his half brother. He had told Julie once that his mother came to Clarkson from somewhere in California when Luis was a baby. Angel knew nothing of her background and didn't even know who his father had been. Julie secretly wondered if the reason his mother had always refused to talk about him was because she didn't know, herself.

Julie was looking forward to the fiesta with mixed feelings. It would be wonderful to see the center open at last, but social events always made her a little nervous. Granted, this would be like nothing she'd ever attended before, and she had made several friends since she started working there, but the idea of spending most of the day and evening around Angel in such a social setting was disconcerting. She planned to keep very busy, helping wherever she was needed, until she gained strict control over the awareness of him that plagued her whenever he was near. The last thing she wanted was for Angel to think she was attracted to him again, even if it was proving to be true.

Chapter Five

The day of the fiesta dawned warm and clear. Julie was up early, unable to sleep any longer. After breakfast she baked some cookies to take with her and then ironed the full skirt and cotton blouse she had decided would be suitable—not too fancy to work in, yet feminine enough to give her a measure of self-confidence. She'd planned on wearing flat-heeled sandals, knowing she would undoubtedly be run off her feet, helping with the party that was scheduled to start in the middle of the afternoon and run until everyone went home.

She and seven other people had spent most of the previous day decorating the place. Even Stef had gotten involved earlier. When the day-care room had been completely painted, Connie had remarked that it would be nice to have some large posters to put on the long wall. Remembering Stef's artistic ability, Julie had approached her about the possibility of painting a mural instead. With Angel's blessing, Stef had spent every evening the week before, decorating the plain yellow surface with colorful animals, birds, flowers and butterflies. It was just the finishing touch the main day-care room needed.

Stef would probably be at the fiesta later on. Angel himself had encouraged her to come, and to bring a friend if she wanted. Julie knew she had planned to ask the fellow worker she'd been seeing. He'd taken her bowling two weeks before, and they had gotten into the habit of eating their lunch together at work.

The telephone rang when Julie was about to leave, having changed her clothes and grabbed her purse and a light sweater.

"Need a ride?" Angel's familiar voice asked after she'd said hello.

His offer surprised Julie, who took a deep breath before answering. He'd been pleasant but distant at work, and she had assumed that he'd made the adjustment to their being together every day, an adjustment she was still struggling to reach.

"I was just leaving."

"That's what I figured. So am I, and I thought you might want a ride. I don't live that far away."

"I know." Silently Julie cursed her wayward tongue. If he ever found out that she'd driven by his house to gawk, she would die of embarrassment. "I mean, that's what I heard."

"You're welcome here any time." His deep voice sent shivers up her arms and across the back of her neck. "I'll give you the ten-cent tour."

She didn't know how to respond to his surprising offer, so she ignored it. "Think we'll have a big turnout today?"

"Judging from the number of flyers I've seen posted, I'd be surprised if we didn't. It was Juan's idea to put 'free food' in big letters."

"That should do it," Julie agreed. "I hope we raise a lot of money."

"About the ride to the center," he urged. "Do you want me to pick you up?"

Angel found himself holding the receiver tightly while he waited for her answer. Julie had been on his mind a lot lately, and he didn't like it at all. Perhaps if he spent a little time alone with her he would be disillusioned, and the unwanted longings would fade.

"That would be nice," she said. "When will you be here?"

Angel was so surprised at her acceptance that he almost dropped the phone. "I'll leave now if you're ready."

"Okay. See you in a few minutes."

"Sure. Bye."

All the way over to her house he wondered what she was playing at. Then he remembered that it had been his idea to offer the ride in the first place. He flexed the fingers that held the steering wheel in a death grip. Today was an important one; the center was opening, and he prayed that it would be a tremendous success. So far everything had fallen nicely into place, and when the day's events were over Julie would be riding home with him.

He didn't allow himself to dwell on that as he pulled into the driveway of her parents' house. One of the big front doors opened and she slipped out, wearing a full, blue skirt and a peasant blouse with a scoop neckline. In one hand she was holding a plate covered with plastic wrap.

He leaped out to open her door.

"Good morning," he said, smiling. "Are those chocolate chip cookies?" She used to make them for him when they were in school.

Her gaze didn't quite meet his as she slid into the passenger seat. "Butterscotch. Thanks for picking me up."

"No problem." He shut her door carefully and got back behind the wheel. This was a different Julie, one he hadn't seen in a long time. She wasn't the poised young socialite from the dance, or the dedicated worker at the center; this woman beside him looked softer, younger. Perhaps more approachable.

The full skirt emphasized her slim waist and swirled around the delicately curving calves that had drawn his gaze when she got into the car. He turned to study her more closely, watching with interest as the pink in her cheeks deepened.

"Aren't we going?"

The silence clearly flustered her.

"In a minute." He liked the way her hair waved softly around her face. He was tempted to touch it, to investigate the silky strands and breathe in its faint scent. For a moment he allowed his gaze to rest on her lips, but she shifted restlessly, and he was reminded that she was no longer his to touch whenever he wanted. Strange how he kept forgetting the years they'd been separated whenever he looked at her mouth.

"You didn't have to bring anything." He glanced down at the tray on her lap.

"I wanted to. I like to bake."

"You look very nice." The words sounded ridiculously tame to his ears as he shifted gears and pulled into the street, thinking how he would have liked to comment on her hair, her skin, the tempting length of her legs. If he didn't stop thinking of her in those terms he was going to run into trouble.

"So do you."

Julie was studying his black jeans and matching shirt, which had the sleeves rolled back and the first two gray pearl snaps at the neck unfastened. The collar was turned up, brushing against Angel's hair. He liked black and wore it often.

He flashed her a smile as their eyes met, excitement flowing through him. When he'd walked away from racing after the terrible accident that had killed one of the other drivers, totaled Angel's car but left him without a scratch, he hadn't thought he would ever feel this alive again. The accident had forced him to think about his own mortality and what was really important. The idea of returning to Clarkson to set up a center for his people had taken root then, and now that dream was becoming a reality. His one big regret on this day was that Luis wouldn't be here for the opening festivities.

Julie had worked hard, and Angel was grateful for her presence. He glanced at her, noticing the way the gold hoops in her ears danced in the sunlight. "We look good together," he said without thinking.

Her stunned expression wiped away his smile. "Representatives of the center," he added dryly. "What did you think I meant?"

For a moment his words had made Julie think of other things. "I wonder what Connie's wearing," she said, ignoring his question. "Since she's also representing the center."

"I'm sure Connie will look beautiful, she always does." Angel's voice had turned chilly, and Julie didn't reply. She wondered if Connie's brand of dark, voluptuous good looks was what Angel found attractive these days. While he'd been in the limelight he'd run to blondes, she thought bitterly, remembering the photos she'd seen. And redheads. She had secretly followed his career since he'd become a success, even when the publicity surrounding him had caused her pain. A scrapbook full of clippings was hidden in the recesses of her closet at home.

She and Angel were the first ones to arrive at *Casa del Sol*. There was a new sign out front, donated by an older member of the community who was a skilled wood-carver. An Aztec-styled sun, painted in warm red-and-orange tones, was carved into the wood, with neat black lettering below it. The sign was mounted on two thick posts by the front door.

They went inside, and Angel spent a few minutes admiring the brightly colored balloons and streamers as some of the other helpers began to arrive. There was still a lot to do.

"Hey, Julie. How are you?"

She turned at the sound of the familiar voice. "Joey! It's been a long time." She hadn't seen Angel's friend for years, since he had told her that Angel was gone and wouldn't be back. Julie had always known that Joey didn't approve of her, and their meeting now was a little awkward as they stood in the hallway looking at each other.

Joey had matured—from an overweight teenager who worshiped Angel with protective zeal, to a thin, wiry adult with a neatly trimmed mustache and a guarded smile. She knew that he was working for Angel, and he probably still disapproved of her.

Someone called his name and he turned. "See you later," he said to her over his shoulder. Julie knew she wouldn't be seeking him out; he was another painful reminder of the past. She went to find Angel, to see what she should do first.

Angel and Ben had gone into the office to discuss picking up two more cribs that had been donated for the nursery. One of the department stores had offered them seconds, damaged in shipping. Sleeping babies wouldn't care if the finish was scratched or a bunny decal on the outside partially peeled off.

"I thought Luis might be home in time for the fiesta," Ben said as Angel leaned against the corner of his desk and checked over a list of things still to be done.

"I hoped he would, but his release won't be for another week. I was going to drive over then, but he insisted on taking the bus."

Luis was across the state at the men's maximum security prison. Angel had talked to him on the phone, but hadn't been there for months. Luis hated for Angel to see him penned up, so Angel had kept his visits to a minimum, calling or writing instead. But he was eager for the only family he knew to come home and begin a new life in Clarkson, working beside Angel at the center.

Connie appeared in the open doorway, wearing a brightly flowered dress with a gathered skirt. Ben greeted her, then turned to leave.

"I'll go pick up those cribs."

"That makes six," Connie said as she stepped past Ben. "With the bedrolls Carlotta sewed up for the older preschoolers, we'll have room for eighteen to take naps in the afternoons."

Angel returned her happy smile. "That's only a beginning. We hope to have around thirty children eventually." He stood up, the clipboard still in his hand. "Don't forget that the state inspector is coming back Monday morning."

Julie poked her head through the open doorway to greet Connie. "Pretty dress. Did you bring the paper plates and cups? Maria wants to start setting up the buffet table."

"Thanks. I'll get the stuff." Connie slipped from the room, greeting someone outside in a rapid stream of Spanish.

"Do you need me for anything right now?" Julie asked Angel. "If you don't, I can help set up the equipment for the children's games."

Angel forced himself to ignore the way the blouse fabric smoothed over her rounded breasts, but his body had already responded immediately to the direction of his thoughts. "Go ahead. Check back with me when you're done, though."

"Okay." For a moment their gazes locked, and the mirror of his own awareness that Angel saw in Julie's hazel eyes shocked him, fueling his discomfort.

"Save me a dance." He thought if he didn't at least hold her in his arms soon he'd go mad. Then he cursed himself for a fool. Dancing with Julie would deepen the ache, not cure it. Still, at least the attraction he felt was only physical, he told himself, although he was having a devil of a time with it. He wanted her, but not enough to risk being hurt again.

If Julie heard his request, she gave no indication as she went through the doorway to the cupboard by Connie's desk where the games had been stored.

Her hands were shaking as she picked up the stack of boxes. Save him a dance, indeed! She had no intention of getting that close to Angel again. Ever. If he was serious, which she doubted, she'd just have to make an excuse when the time came. Angel was handsome and successful, and there would be plenty of women for him to dance with. By evening he would have forgotten about his request, anyway.

Hours later Julie discovered she'd been wrong about Angel's memory. At twilight, the band set up in the larger of the two day-care rooms. When they began to play, Julie went to listen and to take a break from cleaning up the huge buffet. She stood talking to Stef and her date, Tom Bell.

"You've all done such a terrific job," Stef said, looking around. "This party has been super."

Stef's pale hair was loose around her face, the ends softly curled. Light makeup, that Julie had shown her how to apply, completed the picture.

Standing with his arm around Stef's waist, Tom agreed with Stef's comment. "The food was fantastic," he said, patting his flat stomach as Stef laughed. He was a thin man with a ready smile, and Julie had taken an instant liking to him.

He gave Stef's waist a squeeze and pointed to the far wall. "You did a great job with the mural." The animal figures were barely visible in the dim light.

Stef grinned but didn't reply. Compliments made her uncomfortable. Julie was about to change the subject when she noticed Angel threading his way through the groups of people standing around the dance floor, coming toward her slowly but steadily.

Julie shifted slightly, pretending she hadn't noticed him, although her heartbeat began to speed up at the sight of his tall, lean physique, predatory as a jungle cat as he moved purposefully in their direction. As she surreptitiously watched his progress, he stopped to talk to someone, and she released the breath she'd been holding in a jerky rush.

Then Angel shook his head in apparent response to something, his smile a slash of white as he turned again in her direction. Julie tried to concentrate on what Tom was saying over the boisterous music, but it was no use. Her senses were as alerted to Angel's approach as if she'd had him on radar.

Stef, who had always insisted that Angel was one of the most drop-dead gorgeous males on the face of the earth, was quick to greet him and introduce her date.

"Thank you for including us in your celebration," Stef said as the two men shook hands.

"Thank *you* for the wonderful mural. The kids will love it."

The music swelled around them with an insistent beat, a lively number that had the floor filling up rapidly and Julie unconsciously tapping one foot.

Tom looked at Stef. "Shall we try this?" he asked.

She glanced at the dancers for a minute. "If you're not afraid for your toes," she said finally, following him onto the floor.

"How about you? Are you game?"

Julie tried to form the words of polite refusal she'd rehearsed earlier, but her mind went blank, and all she could think of was the danger and wonder of being close to him again. She looked into his face. His expression was bland, but there was a bright light of challenge in his midnight-blue eyes.

Julie's chin went up, and she accepted the offer as if it were a gauntlet he'd tossed down between them.

"Sure." Her voice was casual, but her knees were quaking as she took the hand he extended. His fingers wrapped around hers, warm and firm as he led her into the sea of gyrating bodies. It was all she could do to relax her grip. At least the number was a fast one. He wouldn't be holding her close.

Without her mind's conscious direction, her feet followed his in one of the familiar patterns they'd practiced many times to the music of an old portable radio. She couldn't help but grin at him as they moved as one. They had always danced well together, each effortlessly anticipating the other's steps. Angel's expression was unreadable as his gaze scorched down her body before returning to her face. Rebelliously Julie threw herself into the dance, rewarded by the glitter in Angel's eyes as his body moved in time with hers.

After a few moments the song ended, and the band went immediately into a ballad. One of the guitar players approached the microphone, his voice deep and rich as he crooned in his native tongue. Julie caught the words "love" and "forever" before her Spanish failed her.

Angel stepped closer, holding out his arms. When Julie didn't retreat, he slipped them around her.

"Come on, babe," he coaxed. "Put your arms around my neck and let the music take you." It was what he used to say when he'd taught her folk dances in the past. The words were the same, but they both knew the meaning behind them was vastly different.

Ignoring the warning pangs that rippled through her, Julie could do nothing but obey. If she hadn't clung to him, she might have fallen, her shaky knees finally giving up. His warmth surrounded her in a protective embrace, and her hands linked behind his head, fingers tangling in the silky strands of his hair. Angel had maneuvered them toward a darkened corner, and they were barely moving as they swayed to the music.

For Julie the noise faded, the people who surrounded them retreating until she and Angel stood in a magic circle. She could feel his cheek against her hair and sense the light caress of his breath. After a moment he gathered her even closer, so close they seemed to share a heartbeat. They were touching from breast to thigh, his masculine strength making her pulse race with the pure ecstasy of being near him. Her head spun dizzily and she forgot to breathe.

Angel's hand swept down her back, tracing the curve of her spine, and she became entangled in a web of shimmering desire.

Just when she thought she couldn't stand it for another moment, the song ended on a plaintive note. As she stepped away, Angel's fingers locked around her wrist.

"Where do you think you're going?" His voice had mellowed, and his eyes were dark with promise. One lock of his hair had fallen across his forehead, and Julie's fingers itched to smooth it back.

The spell he was weaving tightened around her throat like a noose, choking her. She had to get away.

"I have to check on the kitchen. I promised I'd be back to help."

His brows furrowed at her words. "You've done enough tonight."

She tugged at her imprisoned wrist. "I have to go."

The annoyance on his face smoothed into cool disinterest as he dropped her arm, the expression in his eyes going blank. "Run along, then."

His tone was light and she hesitated for a moment. Then she turned, skirt whirling around her. She couldn't be close to him without revealing the depth of the feelings his nearness had aroused. Pushing her way through the crowd, Julie made her escape.

Behind her, Angel stood rigidly, the pain of her rejection slicing through him like a hundred razor blades as his fingers curled into hard fists at his sides. He watched Ben speak to Julie, gesturing toward the crowded floor, but she shook her head and kept going. Perhaps their kind was only good enough to work with—not to dance with. God, how she had changed. Before Angel could retreat himself, Connie came up, tilting back her head to smile into his face.

"How about a dance, boss?"

He looked down at her for a moment, then forced a grin and pulled her into his arms.

"Where's Joey?" he asked. She'd been dancing with his friend earlier.

"Someone drank too much *cerveza* and Joey ran him home."

Angel thought of the iced tubs of Mexican beer. "Joey's always helping people."

They danced in silence for a moment, then Connie spoke again. "He's a nice *hombre*," she said.

Later, when Julie came back upstairs, feet aching and hands rough from the hot water, the crowd had thinned, but Angel and Connie were still dancing. As Julie watched, Angel laughed at something Connie said. The number ended, and Angel escorted Connie from the floor, holding her hand in his.

A wave of jealousy hit Julie so hard it staggered her. Connie was her friend. Angel was her boss. So much for objectivity.

The band went into its closing number as the leader thanked everyone for attending and reminded them of the coffee cans for donations that were by the door and in the kitchen downstairs. All around Julie, people began to move toward the staircase.

Connie came up to say good-night. "I'll regret this in the morning when the kids wake me up early. I'm danced out."

"Tonight was a big success," Julie said, not looking at Angel.

Connie smiled at them both. "I'll see you Monday morning."

Angel's hand closed over Julie's shoulder, and she barely suppressed her shiver of reaction. "I have to wait till everyone else leaves," he said. "It shouldn't be too much longer."

"Okay. I'll be in the kitchen."

Angel did his best to keep his expression blank as he nodded. "I'd better see to the band." They had played for free; he wanted to thank them and to see if they needed any help with their equipment.

It was another hour before the center emptied and Angel could lock the front door and set the new alarm, the donations from both big coffee cans stuffed into an envelope under his arm. His free hand reached out automatically to take Julie's as they stepped off the wide porch and headed to the one car left in the parking lot. Deliberately he shoved aside the disturbing thoughts he'd had earlier.

Her fingers linked with his, and Angel felt the tension between them fade. "Congratulations," she said softly.

"For what?"

She stopped by the Ferrari, looking into his face in the moonlight. "For pulling all this off." She indicated the empty building, dark except for one light burning over the front door. "For being the driving force behind something this wonderful, this important."

Angel shook his head, uncomfortable with her praise. "It wasn't just me," he protested. "It was you, and Connie, and Juan, and Ben..."

"But it was your dream, wasn't it?" she persisted. "Your vision. And you're the one who made it a reality." Her expression was grave. "I'm very proud of you."

The words warmed Angel as no one else's could have. He set the envelope on the hood of the car and caught the back of her head in his hand. "Thank you for understanding," he said quietly.

Bending down, he touched his lips to her forehead in what he meant to be a friendly gesture. Then a stronger emotion took over, and he tipped up her chin with his finger. The light from the moon illuminated Julie's face, and Angel stared into her eyes for a timeless moment. Julie's eyelids fluttered shut and she swayed toward him. Before Angel could debate the wisdom of it, their lips met in a sweet, tender kiss.

As Angel's mouth moved warmly against hers, Julie was flooded with powerful memories. She had always enjoyed his touch, and now his maturity and the assurance that went with it only made him more attractive, more compelling. As she responded he deepened the gentle pressure until she yielded to the insistent caress of his tongue and parted her lips for his welcome intrusion.

The past and the present swirled together in her mind as she returned his kiss, savoring the taste and textures that had once been almost as necessary to her well-being as the very air she breathed. Julie was caught up in a whirlpool of sensation, but before she could even begin to take her fill of him, Angel broke the intimate contact and stepped back.

"It's getting late." As he led her to the car, she wondered if the tremor she'd heard in his voice was a figment of her imagination, or an echo of the need that had claimed her for an instant. Looking into the hard lines of his face, she realized she would never know.

The drive home was made in silence. When they pulled up to her house, Julie slid from the car before Angel could open his door. "Thanks for the ride," she said, peering back at him.

As if he sensed her reluctance to break the delicate spell, Angel merely inclined his head. Julie shut the car door gently and slipped into the house. She could hear the quiet growl of the Ferrari as he drove away.

One morning a week later, Luis arrived and Angel met him at the bus station. Luis was darker, shorter and stockier than Angel, with a full mustache and a cocky light in his brown eyes—but he was family. The two men hugged unself-consciously as Angel fought sudden tears.

"It's good to have you home, Brother." His voice was thick with emotion.

"It's good to be out of the pen."

Luis bent over to pick up his one worn suitcase. He had finally paid the price for the crime he'd sworn he hadn't committed, and Angel was eager for him to settle in at the house and the center. Luis would be a tremendous help, and *Casa del Sol* would give him a new purpose.

"Hey, nice car," Luis said as Angel stopped by the Ferrari and stowed his brother's bag inside.

"Wait'll you see the house. We've got our own pool table, and the garden is something else."

"Garden? Hey, little bro, you sound like a farmer. Any beer in the fridge at this fancy house?"

Angel smiled at Luis as he backed the car out of its slot. "Sure, ice cold. And plenty of food if you're hungry."

Luis didn't answer. He was stroking the black leather upholstery with one hand, a thoughtful expression on his face.

Angel was eager for Luis to see the center, but it was three days before his brother felt like doing more than sleeping, eating and watching television. It was difficult for Angel to stifle his impatience, but he kept reminding himself that Luis needed time to unwind, to adjust.

Finally the day came that Luis ran out of excuses and agreed to go with Angel, who did his best to ignore his brother's noticeable lack of enthusiasm.

"You know I'm missing the game shows," Luis said as they turned onto the gravel road.

"It will be worth it," Angel promised as they pulled to a stop. "This is it."

For a moment Luis was silent as Angel held his breath. "Nice sign. When are you going to paint the place?"

Angel swallowed his disappointment, remembering that it would take a while for Luis to lose the hard edge of cynicism he'd acquired in prison.

"This summer," Angel said, getting out of the car. "You can help."

They went inside, Angel leading the way to his office. Overhead he could hear children's voices and the sounds of tiny shoes on the linoleum floor. Julie was at her desk, and she looked up as Angel paused in the doorway.

"Got a minute?" he asked. Since the fiesta, he had begun to share more of the center's business with her. Several times the two of them had stayed after Connie and the others left, to discuss a new program or a problem that had come up. Neither he nor Julie had ever spoken about what happened after the fiesta, but Angel felt that they were slowly, cautiously, building a friendship. Sometimes the idea pleased him, but at other times, when she smiled a certain way or they accidentally touched, it wasn't nearly enough.

Julie stood and circled the desk, leaning against the front of it. "Sure," she said in a light tone. "What's up?"

Proudly Angel led Luis into her office and made introductions. He wanted everyone to like his brother, but it was especially important to him that Luis and Julie like each other.

"You got good taste, little bro."

Angel's half brother was nothing like what Julie had imagined. Luis's hair was as dark as Angel's but lacked its silky texture. His eyes were brown, and his nose rather flat in a square face. His height was a surprise; he only topped her by a few inches. The sleeves of his T-shirt were rolled up high to reveal the bulging muscles of a dedicated weight lifter, and tattoos decorated his forearms. Black leather straps were buckled onto both wrists.

As she shook his outstretched hand, Luis's full lips widened into a smile.

"Pleased to meet you," Julie said automatically as he continued to look her over.

Angel stood behind him, and Julie was sure he was unaware of the direction of Luis's gaze. She tried her best to keep a friendly expression on her face, but something about the man made her uneasy. She firmly brushed aside her reservations. Just because there wasn't a speck of family resemblance between the two men gave her no reason to form hasty conclusions.

"Luis will be working with us here at the center, as soon as he's settled in," Angel said over his brother's shoulder.

Julie could understand Angel's excitement at finally having family with him. His mother had meant the world to him, and her sudden death had brought Angel to his knees. Julie hoped fiercely that Luis wouldn't disappoint him.

"Don't push me, bro," Luis said. "I gotta unwind for a while, you know?" He looked at Julie, and she nodded.

"Of course. You've been away a long time." Realizing what she'd said, she stopped abruptly. "I only meant—"

"That I was in stir." Luis's laugh was a harsh sound. "It's no secret."

There was an awkward pause.

"I'll be looking forward to working with you," she said with renewed determination. "But if you two will excuse me now, I do have some phone calls to make."

Angel turned, but Luis hesitated. "Okay," he said finally. "You and I got lots of time to get to know each other."

He turned away before Julie could formulate a reply, dismayed by how negatively his comment struck her. Gratefully she shut the adjoining door and studiously ignored the sound of their voices as she reached for her telephone list.

Luis came in several times that week, but Julie noticed that he only made a pretext of doing anything constructive when Angel was there. The rest of the time he hung around Connie and herself, who both tried hard to be pleasant and to ignore his off-color jokes. Julie kept reminding herself that he probably didn't have many friends, having been gone for twelve years.

Still, despite Julie's best efforts, his presence made her nervous, and his heavy-handed attempts at flirtation reminded her of the way Brad had liked to bait her when he'd been drinking. She was beginning to feel sorry for Angel, who obviously saw no flaws in Luis. Sooner or later Angel was bound to notice that no one else held anywhere near his high opinion of Luis, who almost always reeked of beer and had a cigarette in his mouth.

"What do you do for excitement?" Luis asked her one day as she was trying to check over the tutoring schedule. "You got a boyfriend?"

Julie looked up, striving for patience. "Not at the moment."

"I thought maybe you had something going with my *hermano* again."

Silently Julie counted to ten. "Your brother is my boss."

"He used to be more."

How much had Angel told him? "That was a long time ago."

"You're the reason he left here."

Julie's patience was stretched so thin she thought it would snap like an old rubber band. "No, he left because he didn't think he had a future in Clarkson." Her lips clamped shut on any further explanation. No way would she discuss that wretched parting with this man, or anyone else. It had cost her too much.

Luis leaned over her desk, his square hands flat against its surface. "I got lots of free time," he said. "I get bored."

Julie didn't know what to say. "I have a lot of work here," she stammered. "It keeps me very busy."

Luis straightened with a grin and a shrug. "No problem." Maybe Julie had misunderstood his intentions. "I'll be back later. I got things to do."

Before Luis could leave, the front door slammed, followed by the sound of Angel's booted footsteps coming toward them.

Luis stuck his hands into the pockets of his low-slung jeans, an unreadable smile curving his mouth, and Julie forced herself to relax.

"Hi," Angel said, sticking his head through the open door. "You two getting better acquainted?"

Chapter Six

For once Julie was happy to be away from the center, away from the pressure of trying to avoid Luis and keep her growing dislike of him hidden from Angel. She shut the front door of her parents' spacious home behind her and crossed the living room, looking for her mother.

She was in the dining room, setting a shallow silver bowl of rhododendrons in the middle of the oval table. When Julie went into the room, Phoebe Remington stepped back to admire the huge blossoms.

"Hello, darling. Isn't 'Spring Dawn's' color marvelous this year?"

"Yes, lovely." Julie barely spared the brilliant flowers a glance. "I found a place and it's perfect."

She had just paid the rent on a one-bedroom apartment not too far from the center and had rushed home afterward to share her news.

"It's partially furnished and freshly painted," she said. "Not far from the center, and I can move in this weekend." She anxiously searched her mother's face to see how her news was going over.

"It's in an older section of town, then?"

"Yes, but the neighborhood's not a bad one. Would you be able to help me pick up some things?"

"I'd love to. We'll miss you here at the house, but I suppose it's time you were on your own." Julie had been afraid her mother's feelings would be hurt, but instead her smile was reassuring.

"I hope you don't get lonesome. After the sorority house and then..." Mrs. Remington's voice trailed off for a moment and she glanced away. "Well, you've never really lived alone, you know."

Julie patted her mother's hand. "I'll be fine. How do you think Father will feel about my moving?"

"He's enjoyed having you back, as I have, but we both agreed that it's time for you to make a fresh start. And we'd like to help with whatever you need if you'd let us." Her expression was hopeful.

"I'd like that. There's a kitchen set and a couch already, appliances and some small pieces, but I'll need a bed right away."

"I don't suppose you want the canopy set from your room?"

Julie shook her head. "Not the bed, thanks. But I'd like to borrow the dresser and nightstand."

"Of course." Julie's mother hesitated, clearing her throat. The outward sign of nervousness surprised Julie, who was used to her unshakable poise.

"Julianna, dear, while we're talking, there's been something I've wanted to say to you for a long time." Her eyes grew moist, and she blinked several times, her chin going up a notch. "If your father and I had had any idea what Bradley was putting you through . . ."

"I know. It's okay, really. For a long time I thought it was my fault, and I just couldn't talk about it." The abuse had started with a shove, then a slap, and all of Brad's repeated promises to change meant nothing. Julie couldn't suppress a shudder when she remembered how dark and twisted his face had been during their last fight, when he had tried to strangle her in a drunken rage.

Her mother's voice coaxed Julie away from the painful memories. "Is it getting any easier?"

"Yes. I stopped really caring for Brad a long time before I actually left." Guiltily she pushed aside the knowledge that she had never really loved him. Maybe that was why she had felt so responsible when things went wrong. "My job's been a big help. I feel like I'm really doing something important."

She had already instructed her first class of tutors, and they in turn were working with eager students.

Her mother spoke again, interrupting Julie's wandering thoughts. "Then I am eternally grateful to your center. I must confess, though, the idea of your being around that ex-convict makes me nervous. Wasn't a man shot during the holdup he committed?"

"Yes, one of the guards, but I'm sure Luis is trying very hard to get his life in order."

Mrs. Remington looked skeptical.

Julie hastened to reassure her. "It will work out. Angel wouldn't let him get anywhere near the center if he thought Luis would cause trouble." Julie wished she could be more certain of that, but Angel had a blind spot where Luis was concerned. She never knew quite how to take the remarks the older brother was always making. They seemed innocent enough, but there was an undercurrent to them that made her uncomfortable.

"You know, your father and I never blamed you for the divorce," her mother said suddenly. "We were disappointed, but only for you."

Julie was surprised. She had felt that the failure of her marriage had been a terrible letdown to her parents.

She knew that not confiding in them until after the separation had hurt them deeply, and she tried to explain why she had kept up a front for so long. "While I was with Brad, whenever he would get angry, I always thought that if I had done something differently, been a better wife—"

"No!" Her mother's eyes blazed with emotion. "That's not true. Brad is a sick man, and you mustn't blame yourself." Her chin was set with determination. "I mean it, Julianna. *Don't ever blame yourself.*"

The words permitted some weight to slide from Julie's shoulders. She had long ago come to accept the idea that there was nothing she could have done differently, but hearing her mother confirm it meant a great deal.

"Well," Julie said, her smile shaky, "when can you go shopping with me?"

The two of them spent three evenings picking things out for the new apartment. Julie was moving on Saturday, and she had the telephone and utilities transferred the day before.

"Here's my new address and telephone number," she told Connie, holding out a piece of paper before leaving *Casa del Sol.* "Effective tomorrow." Julie had deliberately waited until Angel was out of the office to give the receptionist the information, feeling slightly self-conscious about finally leaving the nest.

"Need any help? My cousin has a pickup truck."

"Thanks, but my dad is bringing a truck home from work, and I really don't have that much to move. I'll be unpacked and settled by dinnertime."

She heard Angel's voice down the hallway and hastily changed the subject to what office supplies she needed Connie to order for the next week. When she passed by him, he wished her a good weekend, his friendly smile evoking memories of weekends that had dragged because they could find no way to be together, or Sundays spent driving in her car, walking on the beach or just talking and holding hands at their special place by the river. It took a measure of self-control to answer Angel in as casual a tone as he had used.

As it turned out, her estimate of being settled before dinner was an optimistic one. First, the borrowed truck had a flat tire that needed to be fixed, and then the man who had been going to help with the furniture had gotten sick and had to be replaced. By the time they finally got going, the early start became midmorning. The actual moving, except for the few big pieces, was mostly a parade of boxes into the truck and out again at the new place.

Her parents and her father's friend stayed to help arrange the furniture and to visit, finally leaving late in the afternoon after Julie turned down an invitation to come back to the house for dinner. She was eager to be on her own.

Without taking the time to change, she went to the grocery store, happily wandering the aisles, picking up everything from masking tape to canned soup to fill her newly papered drawers and cupboards. After that she had six more bags to unpack, but at least everything else was put away, and as soon as she was done, she planned to take a shower and order a pizza over her new telephone.

Julie had asked Stef to come by, but she had had plans for the evening and had promised to drop over the next day instead. Julie told herself she was too excited to be lonely already, but she wished there was someone to whom she could show off her new apartment. She wondered what Angel would think of her little place, with its mismatched living room furniture, tiny kitchen and bath, and bedroom she'd completely redecorated in light blue and cream.

Julie was stowing perishables in the small refrigerator, humming along with the music from the stereo she'd brought from the big house, when the doorbell rang. Maybe Stef had changed her mind. Wishing she had taken the time to change out of her cutoffs and old T-shirt, Julie went to the front door and pulled it open.

"Surprise!" Connie shouted. "Happy housewarming!"

Behind her were Juan and his wife, Stef, Tom, and Joey, all holding flat pizza boxes and brown paper bags.

Stunned, Julie pulled the door open wider. "Come in, come in. What a great surprise." She glanced over her shoulder, but everything was picked up except for the kitchen. As her friends crowded by, she suddenly noticed Angel standing at the base of the steps, a large bunch of flowers in his hand.

"Looks like we caught you working," he said, glancing at her grubby clothes as he handed her the bouquet. "Welcome to the other side of town."

Julie's stomach did an abrupt nosedive. Keenly aware of her dirty hands and the strands of hair coming loose from that morning's ponytail, she accepted the huge bouquet, her fingers brushing against his.

"Come in," she said. "Last I heard, *you* were living on *my* side of town."

"Touché." His grin was appreciative.

She didn't stop to analyze the feelings rushing through her as she shut the front door behind him. The others in the group were exclaiming over the apartment, opening pizza boxes and putting beer and wine in the fridge.

Julie glanced at the flowers in her hand. "These are gorgeous. I'd better put them in water right away." The carnations, tulips and daffodils filled three vases.

"This place is *attractive*," Connie said, sitting down. "And very cozy."

With an effort, Julie tore her attention from Angel, who was still standing by the door. Perhaps he hadn't meant to stay. Determinedly she showed Connie, Stef and Juan's wife, Sofina, the rest of the apartment as the men gathered in the living room. When the women came out of the bedroom exclaiming over the new brass bed, Angel was still there. They put pieces of pizza onto paper plates and found seats, some on kitchen chairs, as Julie passed out glasses and napkins.

"This is terrific," she said, taking some pizza for herself. "I was just about to order one of these."

The only place left for her to sit was in the middle of the old couch next to Angel. He looked up with a challenging gleam in his eye and patted the cushion beside him. "I won't bite."

"Gotta mind the boss," Juan said as Julie sat down gingerly between the two men. "Have some wine."

After a few minutes Juan rose to get more pizza. The cushion tipped, sending Julie rolling into Angel. Before she could right herself, his arm curved around her shoulders, imprisoning her.

"That's right," he said softly as the others watched with interest. "It never hurts to be nice to the boss."

Julie struggled, flustered.

"Good for you," Connie teased. "Soften him up so he'll okay the new television for the teen lounge."

"What television?" Angel was still looking down at Julie, the warmth of his gaze tempting her to forget all about the other people in the room. The familiar, tantalizing scent of his cologne flooded her senses.

"Never mind that now," Connie said. "I'm sure you'll hear all about it soon enough."

Angel's attention flicked briefly to Connie before returning to Julie, still cradled possessively in the curve of his arm.

"Maybe I'd better stay after the others leave, and you can tell me about it."

His voice was husky, and Julie wondered if he was trying to entertain the others. A quick glance told her that no one was paying any attention.

Angel didn't seem to need a reply, and Julie wasn't sure she could have managed one. A lump had risen into her throat at his surprising suggestion, and his body heat radiated like the warmth of the sun, melting away her ability to form rational thought.

"Connie, can you give Joey a ride home?" he asked over her head.

"Sure," Connie replied.

As Julie glanced first at Joey and then back at Angel, she almost missed the other woman's blush. But Julie didn't miss the thumbs-up sign Joey gave Angel from behind Connie's back. Then she understood why Angel had been so quick in his offer to stay behind.

She was painfully aware that his arm stayed around her as everyone finished up their pizza and wine, drinking from the new glasses they had brought her as a housewarming present. Julie did her best not to lean against him on the saggy couch as he ate, instead making a point of watching the others and occasionally interjecting a remark.

Connie presented her with handwoven place mats for the kitchen table, and Stef and Tom had brought a small watercolor of a ferryboat pulling into the terminal at Anacortes. Stef had painted it, and Tom had done the matting and framing.

When Julie leaned forward to examine the gifts, Angel dropped his arm. She missed its warmth.

"Well," Tom said after a few more minutes, glancing at his watch, "it's time Stef and I got going or we'll miss the movie."

His remark caused a general exodus. Julie stood up, following the others to the door and thanking them as she stole a quick glance over her shoulder. Angel was still sitting comfortably on the couch, sipping his wine. One foot was propped on the other knee, revealing a beautifully worked cowboy boot in silver-gray leather beneath the leg of his black jeans.

Taking a deep breath, she said a last goodbye, shut the door and leaned against it. "So," she said brightly, "what do you think of the apartment?"

Angel stood and crossed the small room, which suddenly seemed to shrink. Once, the two of them would have considered the chance to be alone together a special gift, and she remembered with a wave of heat how they would have spent the time. She watched his approach warily.

"It's very homey." His velvety voice reached out to entrap her. "But I wonder how long you'll be happy here."

"Why do you say that?"

He scuffed at a worn spot in the rug with his toe. "It's not your usual style."

Julie allowed her gaze to sweep him from head to foot, taking in his blue suede shirt and expensive jeans. "We all change."

His eyes narrowed. "Not underneath where it counts."

Surprised by the underlying bitterness in his voice, Julie moved so that a small table was between them.

"I really need to shower and get cleaned up. Can't our discussion wait until Monday?"

Angel forced himself to remain motionless as he watched her nervous retreat. For a while, seated with the group, he'd let his mind wander back to the time that Julie had been his. Now reality came crashing back as they stared at each other across the small expanse of living room.

"Sure, but there's something else I wanted to ask you." He raked a tired hand through his hair. "If you could spare me another moment?"

"Of course." Julie dropped into a straight chair.

Angel had wanted to give Joey the opportunity to be alone with Connie, but he also had legitimate business to discuss with Julie. Now was as good a time as any.

"I have to attend a dinner in Seattle Thursday evening, and I'd like you to go with me."

"What kind of dinner?" Her expression was puzzled.

"The Evergreen Women's Professional Organization. They're considering a donation to the center, and they'd like to look us over first. Since they specifically asked about the literacy program, I need you with me."

Actually, the people they would be seeing didn't even

know about the literacy program, but Angel thought it added a convincing touch to his argument.

Despite his success, he still felt sometimes as if he'd come in the back door and would be found out at any moment. Having Julie at his side would take away that feeling.

She relaxed visibly. "Of course I'll go. You should know by now that I'd do anything for the center."

Angel rose and headed toward the door. No point in pushing his luck. "Thanks. We can discuss the details at work."

"Thank you again for the lovely flowers."

He turned. "Do you remember how we used to drive through the fields when the tulips were in bloom in that little red Mustang you had?" In the spring the floor of the Skagit Valley turned into a carpet of flowers.

"I remember." For a moment her expression gentled. "The flowers you brought tonight reminded me of those rows of color."

Angel took a step forward before he could reconsider. "And their beauty reminds me of you."

Awareness bloomed between them, its petals unfolding into the sudden silence as Angel looked into Julie's face. His heart seemed to stop, then its beat resumed in double time, sending the blood pounding in his ears. His arms reached for her. He was barely conscious of her hands sliding around his neck as he bent to cover her mouth with his. For a moment the past surrounded them, passion exploding within him as Julie fit her lips to his.

Her satiny warmth was all he remembered and more. Caught up in a rush of desire, Angel stroked her mouth with his tongue. Her lips parted on a moan, and a harsh sound of need worked its way up from his throat as he plunged his tongue inside.

Eagerly he explored the silky depths, savoring her unique taste before his tongue met Julie's in a fiery caress. Her tentative response caused Angel's arms to tighten convulsively as he pressed his aroused body tight against her softness. His mind spun with memories of her body under his, memories that had intruded whenever he had tried to find solace elsewhere.

Desire turned to hunger, and hunger to burning need. As Julie returned his kisses, her fingers tangled in his hair, urging him closer. Angel's hand locked her to him as its mate slid a caress from her waist to her breast. The rounded weight fit more fully into his palm than he remembered; she had flowered while he had been gone. With another groan, he thrust jealousy aside, his fingers finding and stroking her hardened nipple.

Instantly Julie stiffened.

The red haze of passion receded slowly as he realized she had stopped responding. Placing one last kiss on the side of her throat, Angel drew in a shuddering breath and loosened his embrace. With unflattering haste, Julie pulled away.

"I want you." He couldn't hold back the words.

Julie's face was flushed, her eyes dark with reaction. "We can't let this happen again," she said. Emotion laced her shaky voice.

Her words, along with his own returning common sense, doused the fire in Angel's blood. What had he been thinking? His heart might be safe, but his body craved her with a scorching hunger that could consume them both if he wasn't careful.

"I'd better go." Without another word, he went out the front door, leaving her standing silently behind him.

If he had trouble sleeping tonight, it would be his own fault. If he had any sense, if he had learned anything at all, he would leave Julianna Remington strictly alone and find someone else to take the edge off his passion.

Behind him, Julie's thoughts were running along different tracks to the same conclusion. She sank to the couch, dismayed by a devastating realization. No wonder she had been unable to give Brad the love that might have helped him to change his destructive ways. Her heart, her very soul, had always belonged to Angel, and to her utter despair, it still did.

The knowledge that he desired her was cold comfort. How could she care for a man she couldn't trust not to desert her again? Once before he'd left her behind after swearing on his mother's memory that he couldn't live without her.

He offered nothing but heartache, and she would be wise to keep her distance. The only thing that had changed was that now Angel was even less vulnerable to her than he had been before. A tear trickled down Julie's cheek as she looked at the vases of flowers he'd brought, feeling more alone than she ever had in her life.

Julie was in one of the downstairs classrooms giving an orientation talk to several prospective tutors when Angel slipped into the back of the room. His morning had been filled with appointments, and he had collected some much-needed pledges.

Glancing up briefly, Julie went on with her speech, determined not to be affected by his presence. It was as if her response to his kisses had been a demented dream.

"There is no gift so precious as teaching someone to read," Julie was saying. "The time you give of yourselves will be returned a hundredfold in appreciation and gratitude. Your own lives will be enriched, and you will be opening up unlimited possibilities to those you teach.''

Angel put his feet up on the chair in front of him and rubbed a hand across his face. Despite the morning's success, he was tired and edgy. He'd had an argument with Luis when he'd stopped by the house on the way back to the center. Angel had wanted Luis to come with him, but his brother seemed content to spend his days drinking beer and watching television. When Angel pushed, Luis muttered something about getting his hands on some real money and blowing the town for good. Hurt, Angel had slammed out of the house.

He would have to be more patient with his brother. Luis just needed more time.

Julie paused in her talk, looking into the faces of each person in the small audience. Angel was surprised to see that several of them were Anglos.

''We ask that you make a real commitment, but the schedule you set up is between you and your student. The more time you can give, the faster the progress.''

Her voice went on, shimmering with enthusiasm, her dedication evident. In the short time that *Casa del Sol* had been open, the reading program had grown tremendously. Pleased, Angel took a deep breath as some of his tension and fatigue drained away, lulled by the music in her voice.

Behind him the door opened wider.

''Boss,'' Connie whispered. ''The upstairs toilet is plugged again.''

Later that same evening Julie thrust aside the sheaf of papers she'd been checking, trying to match applicants to tutors. Connie had left half an hour before, and Julie needed to go to the grocery store on the way home. Soon the center would be bustling with evening classes, as it was almost every night, so she had better make her getaway while the coast was clear.

Closing the door behind her, she looked into Angel's office, but it was empty. She hadn't seen him since he'd followed Connie out of the orientation talk earlier. Disappointed, she started to leave, but the faint sound of his voice stopped her. It was coming from the partially finished teen lounge. Silently she crept toward the door that was ajar, and listened.

"Marco, you have to stay in school. It's the only way you'll break the pattern. You don't want to end up in the fields like your folks and your older brother, do you?"

Julie could hear Angel clearly.

"What's wrong with the way my folks live?" asked a voice filled with defensiveness and pain.

"Nothing, man. But don't you want more?"

"I can make good money at the refinery. I want to help."

"Yes, but you'll only be kept on as long as the shutdown lasts. When the maintenance work is finished, you'll be down the road." Angel's voice had an edge of impatience, and Julie could feel his frustration. "You need to stay in school or you'll always be the first man they let go."

"Aw, you did okay. You cut out before graduation, and look at you now."

Julie strained to hear as Angel's voice went low.

"I know I did okay, but I took a lot of stupid chances. Guys *die* doing what I did. And I paid a price."

The boy he was talking to sounded puzzled. "What price? I heard you had nothin' here, that your old lady was killed in a brawl at The Schooner."

There was a long silence, and Julie ached for the pain that that reminder must bring Angel.

"I made a mistake when I ran away. I wanted to leave my problems behind. Instead I lost something precious to me. Something irreplaceable. Take my word for it, Marco. Stay in school. There are no real shortcuts."

His voice stopped, and Julie could picture him groping for a way to reach the boy, even if it meant exposing more of his own pain. Tears gathered behind her lashes.

"I may have found success and made a lot of money, but it wasn't worth the price. Why do you think I came back?"

"The newspaper said you got scared, lost your nerve. That ain't true, is it?"

Guilt at listening to something so private finally made Julie start to turn away, when Angel spoke again. "If you try to beat the odds like I did, you end up paying. That's why I came back here. I haven't stopped paying for running away."

Marco started to speak again, but Julie tiptoed quietly away. Tears streamed down her face, for the boy Angel had been and the mother he had lost. Tears for her own loss of faith and innocence, too. How could Julie trust in Angel or anyone, after her disastrous marriage had made a mockery of love?

The evening of the dinner, Julie was getting ready with one eye on the clock, not wanting to keep Angel waiting when he got there. He had warned her that the evening was a formal occasion, and she had chosen to

wear a new dress, a long mint-green creation with full
sleeves and a matching vest covered with pearlescent
sequins. The bodice of the dress was low, revealing the
upper curves of her breasts, and the softly pleated skirt
flowed over her hips like a waterfall, shimmering when
she walked. With it, Julie wore pearl teardrop earrings
and a matching pendant on a fine gold chain. Since the
late spring nights in western Washington could be chilly,
she pulled a white wool coat from the closet. Her
mother had offered the loan of a fur for the evening,
but Julie disapproved of wearing them and had politely declined.

She was twisting around in front of the full-length
mirror in her bedroom, critically examining her up-
swept hair when the doorbell rang. Taking a deep
breath, she scooped up her evening bag and went to
answer it.

The sight of Angel in his tuxedo affected her as
strongly as it had at the country club dance. The black
and white clothing was a perfect foil to his honey-tan
skin and dark hair.

"Come in." She pulled the door wide and stepped
aside, but he still remained on the porch, looking at her.

"You're a vision," he said finally.

Flushing with pleasure, Julie thanked him. "It's no
strain to look at you, either. There's something about a
man in evening clothes..." Her voice trailed off as he
stepped past her and turned.

"For God's sake, Julie, don't stop now." His voice
had taken on a teasing tone. "All week I've been begging for money and unplugging toilets. The only women
to pay me compliments have been two feet tall and under five years old."

Julie knew he tried to visit the preschoolers on the second floor of the center every day, and they all loved him.

"A man's ego can only take so much," he continued. "Tell me more."

The width of his shoulders beneath the smooth cut of his jacket was distracting, but Julie did her best to go along with his playful mood. "Good teeth are always an asset," she said in a demure voice.

"Is that the best you can do?"

Tapping a finger to her chin, she circled him. "Well, your shoes have an admirable shine."

Angel threw up his hands in disgust. "Your skills of flattery are definitely rusty. Maybe you can refine them on the way to Seattle. I'd hate to think you might tell one of our potential sponsors that she has good teeth."

"I'll do my best to rise to the occasion," she said as Angel helped her on with her coat. "Perhaps you could give me a few examples of what you mean."

Angel's hands settled on his hips and he backed away, studying her critically while Julie tried not to squirm.

"You look like a fairy princess in that dress," he said reverently. "Your eyes sparkle like priceless gems, your skin has the glow of porcelain, your body—" He kissed the tips of his fingers, eyes gazing heavenward. *"Bellissimo."*

Embarrassed, Julie laughed. "You're not Italian."

"But you know how bad my Spanish is. Anyway—" his eyes gleamed with appreciation "—you get the idea."

"Yes, I think I have it now."

"Why don't you practice on me after we get in the car? We'd better be going."

Their friendly banter lasted most of the ninety-minute ride to Seattle. After they had exhausted their supply of outrageous flattery, they started discussing mutual acquaintances. From there the conversation drifted to other pleasant topics. As Angel pulled into the parking garage of a restaurant in Seattle's north end, Julie was surprised at how fast the drive had gone.

She took Angel's arm as they walked across the lobby and up the stairs to the room where the dinner was being held. Angel appeared to be unaware of the attention they were getting, but Julie couldn't help but be pleased by the feminine stares directed at her escort.

When they reached the open doorway to the banquet room and Julie peered inside at the sea of round tables, an older woman rushed up to greet them.

"Mr. Maneros, we're so glad you could make it. I'm Glenda Johnson."

Angel introduced Julie, who returned the other woman's polite greeting.

"I want you to meet some people before you take your seats at the head table." She pointed to the dais with a flutter of her hand.

Julie stopped in her tracks, tugging on Angel's arm. "What's going on here?" she whispered.

The woman with them must have heard. She glanced at Angel, then back at Julie with a puzzled look on her face. "Surely you told Ms. Remington that you're our guest speaker tonight." She directed her gaze to Julie. "We're all looking forward to hearing about Mr. Maneros's exciting career as a race car driver."

Chapter Seven

"What about the center?" Julie asked. "I thought we were here to discuss that."

"Center?" Glenda Johnson echoed.

Angel's fingers squeezed Julie's warningly. "Let's talk about this later."

Julie glanced at the other woman's quizzical expression and then back at Angel, pursing her lips thoughtfully. "It had better be good."

Angel smiled as he turned to their escort. "You wanted to introduce us to someone?"

Glenda Johnson's curiosity was no match for his considerable charm. "Right this way," she said with a trill of laughter. "Let's swing by the bar and get you something to drink first."

By the time they had met and mingled with what Julie was sure must be most, if not all, of the people attending the function, she'd become thoroughly impressed with Angel's ability to introduce *Casa del Sol* into each conversation. One moment they were discussing his racing career, the next, Julie's job as head of the adult literacy program. Or the need for a larger daycare program. Or a scholarship fund Angel wanted to establish to aid Chicano students attending the local community college.

As they moved through the crowd, his hand lingered at Julie's back, fingers slipping beneath the hem of the sequined vest to lightly caress the skin bared by the dress's daring cut. Whenever Julie glanced at his face, his eyes glowed back at her with a warmth that she would have labeled possessive, making it increasingly difficult for her to come up with correct, even coherent responses to the many questions about her duties. Having Angel smile down at her approvingly was heady stuff, and Julie had to concentrate hard not to make an inappropriate remark.

"What's it like working with a celebrity?" a young woman asked her, casting a melting glance at Angel.

Julie's smile never wavered as she gave in to sudden impulse. "It's exciting. A daily thrill."

When Angel glanced at her, she fluttered her lashes at him, secretly pleased at his embarrassed expression.

"He's just the best boss," she cooed.

The blonde sighed. "I can imagine."

Julie almost choked with laughter at the other woman's adoring tone and Angel's shrug of discomfort.

The woman reached out to shake his hand. "You're a real hero," she said with feeling.

Julie watched with interest as dusky color crept up Angel's high cheekbones. "Thank you."

"Time to take your seats, I think," Glenda Johnson said, coming to rescue them. Julie turned to follow her to the raised head table, but Angel's fingers locked around her wrist, pulling her up short as he leaned close to her ear.

"If you ever refer to that little exchange again, you will be in serious trouble," he told her in a threatening tone.

"Me? I'm too impressed to say anything." Laughter bubbled in Julie's throat, but she fought to suppress it.

"Behave," Angel whispered, "or I'll give you a *thrill* you aren't expecting."

"It's in the hero's handbook," Julie shot back. "You aren't allowed to make threats."

Angel rolled his eyes wordlessly, schooling his features as they caught up with Glenda, who was waiting to introduce them to the women already seated on the dais. Julie watched with interest as Angel switched effortlessly back to the role of sophisticated celebrity.

Moments later, when his hand closed abruptly over her knee, his warmth soaking through the sheer fabric of her long skirt, Julie waited impatiently for the woman on her right to finish speaking before turning to him.

Angel tugged at his collar, looking for a moment as if he would rather be wearing an old sweatshirt. "If some of the promises I got for donations come through, added to the fee I'm getting for speaking tonight, we'll have money for the new television and VCR for the teen lounge, the assistants we need to expand the day-care center, and some left over for a sizable contribution to our regular budget," he told her in a low voice.

Julie leaned closer. "How much are they paying you?" she asked quietly.

When he told her, she was shocked. "I had no idea your words were worth so much. And here you've been talking to me for free," she teased.

"Don't get sassy. Evenings like this one will keep the *Casa*'s doors open, and that's what we're both working for, right?"

"Do these people know what they're getting?" she couldn't help but ask. "Here they are expecting to be entertained by Angel Maneros, champion daredevil race car driver and poster pinup, and instead you're planning to relieve them of their tax-deductible dollars." Julie glanced out at the audience seated before them, then back at Angel. "They may get ugly."

He smiled at her disrespectful description. "Don't worry. They'll get their money's worth." His voice deepened, accent suddenly thick. "I c'n talk good for da big bucks."

Julie slapped at his arm. "You'll set the cause back a hundred years."

"Oh, yeah? Watch me. I'll dazzle 'em."

Of that she had no doubt.

"You should have been a door-to-door salesman," she whispered. "You'd have made a fortune."

"Why didn't you tell me that before I risked my butt racing cars?"

His expression was so comically indignant that Julie burst into laughter, quickly stifling it with her hand as the woman next to her bent forward to look at them both.

"That reminds me," Angel said as she took a sip of water, "I'll be leaving for a week sometime soon."

Julie's fingers tightened dangerously on the goblet. A whole week! "Where are you going?"

"I have to fly to New York. It's time to do the new campaign for Dark Angel cologne. They've promised to get the television and print ads done in one trip, but I'm not sure of the exact dates yet."

Julie leaned back as the waiter set a salad in front of her. Sometimes she was able to forget that Angel was much more than the devastatingly attractive head of a Chicano community center in a small town in the Skagit Valley. Then something would happen to bring back his celebrity status. She could feel the heat rise in her cheeks when she thought of how she had been teasing him.

This was the man whose face had been on the cover of many national magazines, and she had told him he would have made a good door-to-door salesman! She shifted away self-consciously, picking up her fork and scowling at the plate of salad greens before her.

"You aren't upset, are you? Connie will help to handle things while I'm gone, and Luis will be around if you need him."

"No problem." Julie impaled a cherry tomato with her fork. The center could burn down before she'd ask Luis for help. With Angel out of town, he would undoubtedly be a bigger pain than usual.

The woman on Angel's other side, who had been introduced as the organization's president, touched Angel's sleeve and asked him a question. While he responded, Julie glanced briefly at the silky hair that brushed his collar, remembering how it felt slipping between her fingers. The resolutions she had made about her feelings toward Angel weren't holding up very well so far. The waiter took her salad plate and Julie turned her attention to the lawyer on her right.

They chatted through the Polynesian chicken and rice, and by dessert the lawyer had expressed an interest in touring the center. Hoping it might lead to another donation, Julie gave the woman her card.

"Call anytime," she said over the white chocolate mousse.

As soon as the dishes were cleared away and coffee poured, the president rose to introduce Angel. Watching his relaxed pose, Julie remembered how in high school he dreaded oral reports but refused to let his nervousness show. Sheer strength of will had overcome his shyness then, and life in the public eye had doubtlessly polished his style.

"Now let me present the man you'd much rather hear speak than me," finished the president, "Angel Maneros."

He pushed back his chair and stepped to the podium, accompanied by a resounding burst of applause and one exuberant wolf whistle.

"Thank you very much," he said, bowing in the direction of the shrill salute. A wave of appreciative laughter followed. As soon as it began to die down, he mentioned how glad he was to be there and launched into his talk.

Beside him, Julie listened with interest as he discussed the early days of his driving career, working in the pits and scrambling to get a ride in a race car. His words filled in some of the blanks about his life away from Clarkson. It hadn't all been glamour and success, at least not at the beginning.

The stories he told about his later years were sprinkled with the names of famous sports figures and entertainers, and the audience's attention was riveted on him when his voice turned serious and he brought up the accident that turned his footsteps homeward. As far as Julie knew, he had never commented on it publicly before.

"My friend was dead, my car was totalled and I walked away with a few scratches and a sprained wrist." Angel glanced down at Julie before he continued, his expression remote. Perhaps withholding a tiny part of himself was the only way he could deal with the tragedy.

"I had an opportunity not many of us are given," he continued, "a chance to rethink my life, to reassess my goals. I realized then how meaningless it had all become."

His words reminded Julie of what he had told Marco about paying the price.

There wasn't a sound in the room as Angel related how he had gotten the idea for a Chicano center while he was in California. "The idea had taken root in the back of my mind months before the accident," he said. "When it came time for me to test-drive the new car we were building to replace the one that was destroyed, I realized that, for me, racing was over. My heart was no longer in it."

He went on to tell the audience about the turtle the preschoolers at the center had named RV because it carried its house with it, related a success story about a man who had already found a good job through their placement service and taken his family off welfare, and mentioned a teenager who had been kept from dropping out of school. Julie wasn't surprised that he failed to take any credit for that. Pride and admiration welled up in her. These people admired Angel without knowing how far he had come. Julie loved him more because she did.

After a passionate summary of his hopes for the *Casa*'s future, Angel sat down to a final burst of applause.

When the evening was over, it took a while to thread a path across the large room. They could have stayed for another hour fielding questions, but at long last Angel mentioned the long drive they had ahead of them and steered Julie toward the door. When he had gotten her coat and they stepped outside, Angel stopped to look up at the scattered stars.

"Let's walk along the marina for a few minutes," he said. "I need to clear my head." He helped Julie into her coat.

She laid her hand in his warm, rough palm, and his fingers curled around hers protectively, drawing her closer. Wordlessly they descended to the sidewalk that bordered the inky water. The night was pleasantly cool, and a light breeze lifted the loose tendrils of Julie's hair with inquisitive fingers. To one side a steady succession of docks jutted into the water, which was thick with boats. On the other was a steep bank leading back up to the parking lot. Some of the boats glowed with lights, and Julie could hear music and voices as she walked at Angel's side. The notion of sailing away with him on one of the tall-masted beauties teased at her.

With determination she shifted gears. "That was quite an impressive speech."

His shrug brushed along her arm. "I've given various pieces of it many times."

"But not the part about the accident," she said with sudden certainty.

Angel stopped, placing his hands on her shoulders as he studied her upturned face in the faint moonlight. "You always knew me so well," he said softly.

As quickly as that, the mood between them changed, from almost easy to tension-filled. Julie stepped back and he released her.

"Lucky guess," she said in a voice that aimed for lightness and failed.

"Like hell."

"I think it's time we headed back." Suddenly she was chilly in the evening air, and desperate to put some space between them until she could regain her equilibrium.

Her pace quickened as she preceded Angel back toward the car, and she glanced around at him as she went up the steps. At that moment her toe caught in the hem of her long dress and she pitched forward awkwardly.

Angel's arm shot out to grab her. Seeing it swinging toward her, Julie twisted away from him with a shriek, dropping her purse and gripping the metal handrail to keep herself from falling. For a moment the image of Brad's face, dark with rage, intruded.

"Are you okay?"

Julie hugged the railing with both hands, willing the wild trembling to stop. When she had seen his arm swing toward her, she had reacted instinctively, trying to protect herself.

"I'm fine." Even her voice shook.

Angel reached down to pick up her bag and handed it to her. "Mind telling me what that was all about?" he finally asked as she turned to climb the stairs.

"Nothing. I thought I was going to fall." Julie forced the remaining tremors to stop as he took her arm in a light grip. If she was lucky, he would be satisfied with her answer.

Luck wasn't with her.

"I'm a lot of things, but I'm not stupid," he said, breaking the silence as they crossed the parking lot, her elbow in his firm grasp. He released her to unlock the passenger door, but didn't open it immediately.

Refusing to meet his gaze, Julie reached for the door handle herself. Muttering something that sounded like "stubborn female" under his breath, Angel yanked it open.

"Get in." His voice fairly crackled with suppressed violence.

Julie obeyed.

"Now," he said as he slid behind the steering wheel and jammed the key into the ignition, "tell me what the hell is going on."

He was clearly prepared to sit there all night. Julie turned and looked out the side window, lacing her fingers nervously. "I told you, I almost fell."

"Julianna." There was sympathy in his voice, as well as the arrogance of someone who had the right to ask and to expect an answer.

Somehow that goaded her. Swallowing, she started to talk, stumbling at first. No one but her parents had ever heard the whole story about the end of her marriage. As she spoke, something drove her to tell Angel every bitter detail. Maybe, perversely, she just wanted to see how much pity and revulsion she could bring to his face. Maybe she hoped he could somehow miraculously erase the whole, hurting memory.

When she got to the last fight she'd had with Brad and began to describe how he, drunk as usual, had fastened his hands around her throat, tears of reaction filled her eyes and her voice began to shake.

Angel's hand slapped the wheel, making her jump.

"Enough!" His command was a muted roar.

"You wanted to know!" Julie cried, the tears spilling over and cascading down her cold cheeks. "You wouldn't let it alone."

"Oh, baby," he breathed, quieting as suddenly as he had exploded, eyes glittering in the dim light. "I'm so sorry." Gently he pulled her into his arms, laying her head against his wide shoulder. "I'm so sorry."

As he rubbed her back in long, soothing strokes, Julie nestled closer, snuffling against the smooth fabric of his jacket. She could feel the pain, the anger, even the crippling guilt, begin to melt away as Angel talked to her in low, soft tones as if she were a child who needed comfort.

"It wasn't your fault," he said over and over. "It wasn't your fault."

For uncounted moments they held each other, Julie's tears eventually stopping as she listened to Angel's steady breathing, absorbing his special scent and the warmth of his powerful body. After what seemed like a long while, the calm that had soaked through her like a healing drug was replaced by a much more volatile emotion. Nervously she shifted in his embrace.

Angel's arms tightened around her, and Julie thought she detected an increase in his heartbeat. She had become achingly aware of his closeness. Wordlessly she raised her head, looking full into his face, hard as carved stone in the cold, dim light.

When he dipped his head she didn't move. At first the kiss was gentle, almost tentative. Wordless understanding passed between them—acceptance, comfort, peace. Angel lifted his mouth, groaning softly. "I should have been here to protect you."

His words were overwhelming. What did they mean? Did he regret leaving her behind? Greedy for answers, Julie sat up straighter.

"Why did you go?" she asked. "Why didn't you ever get in touch with me?"

Angel frowned as if in pain, shaking his head. "I'd like to get my hands on your ex-husband," he said through gritted teeth. "I bet he's a coward around someone his own size. Most bullies are."

Julie touched his arm. "Angel, did you hear me? Why did you abandon me and never write?"

His attention seemed to come back to her from far away, his narrowed gaze focusing on her face. "What? Are you somehow comparing me to him?"

His question shocked her, and she flinched at the anger in his voice. She had felt so close to him that she thought it might be a good time to discuss the past, to put it behind them. His impatience and lack of understanding shattered her hopes.

"You hurt me more than he ever did!" As soon as the words were out, Julie regretted them.

Angel became still, his eyes turning to ice in his coldly furious face. His lack of expression made Julie shiver, but she couldn't retract the accusation.

"You were the one who backed out," he said in a deadly voice as he started the engine. "You tell *me* about betrayal, lady."

Over the years, Julie had tried not to think about his hurt, carefully nursing her own pain and anger. Now, as he pulled onto the street, his face a mask, she fastened her seat belt and gazed into the night, deep in thoughts of the past.

* * *

"Angel, I can't leave! I'm going to college to be a teacher. You're going to vocational school, and after graduation we're getting married. We agreed."

Angel's hands splayed against his hips as he paced across the trampled grass of their special spot by the river, a muscle jumping in his cheek.

"Julie, grow up. I'll never be anything in this town." He gripped her upper arms and gave her a little shake that widened her eyes. Angel had never touched her with anything but tenderness. "We can *never* be together here. They won't let us."

She turned her head away as if to ward off his words. "You're upset because of what happened to your mother. Give it time. My parents will learn to accept you, I promise."

Angel's determined expression didn't alter as his hands fell away. "Your parents don't even know I exist," he said. "They'd break us up if they did. You were even nervous at my mother's funeral, afraid the wrong person would see you."

He lit a cigarette and drew the smoke into his lungs. "Leaving is our only real chance to be together." He pulled her into his arms, gaze fiercely intense. "Come with me, Julie. I've lost my mother, I can't lose you, too."

How could she refuse when he put it like that? She nodded slowly, sliding her arms around his neck as she shoved aside all her reservations.

Angel buried his head against her shoulder, a deep sigh draining the tension from his young body. "Thank you, babe. You won't regret it, I swear to you."

* * *

Angel had no right to blame her for changing her mind. If he had only been patient and not run off, none of the lost years would have ever happened.

Deep in the pockets of her white coat, Julie's fingers curled into fists. Angel had hurt her once, and like a silly little idiot, she had kept trusting. She had turned to Brad, who had betrayed her, too. She might have to work with Angel, she might want him, but she would be damned if she would let him close enough to wound her again, she vowed silently. Hadn't she finally learned?

He switched on the radio and music filled the air. Through the darkness they drove, each thinking their own thoughts.

Angel was aware from the change in her breathing just when Julie fell asleep beside him. How he longed to pull the car over and take her back into his arms. How he wished they could fall asleep together and wake up side by side. But she had decided their fate years before. When he finally pulled into the parking area in front of Julie's apartment and shut off the engine, she awoke.

Angel watched her as awareness returned. For a moment he looked deep into her eyes before she shuttered them, closing him out. Her defenses were back in place. With a sigh, he opened his door and, stretching his legs, circled the car. His heart was still filled with sorrow and anger over what she had suffered at the hands of her ex-husband. Angel would have loved to spend five minutes alone with Bradley Hammond.

When he opened her door and stretched out his hand, Julie sat looking at him until he finally dropped it and stepped back. She got out unassisted, straightening the long skirt, and glanced at her front door, then back at him.

"It's late. I won't ask you in."

Angel raked a hand through his hair. Maybe she was right. They both needed time apart. "That's okay. I want to drive by the center anyway. Just to check things out."

Her brows arched in surprise. "You do that every night?"

"No. With the alarm I don't have to, but one of the new instructors locked up tonight. Won't hurt to check. Good night."

"Good night. And thank you." She wasn't sure if he would understand what she was thanking him for—the evening or the quiet moments of support in the car. She wasn't really sure herself.

"Yeah." As he turned and the glow from her porch light fell on his tired face, Julie began to have doubts. Perhaps she wasn't the only one who had been hurt when Angel left. He waited politely while she unlocked her front door, and then with a careless wave he drove off.

It was several days later that Luis showed up at the center again, after Angel left for a seminar in Bellingham, a forty-minute drive to the north.

"Hey, pretty lady, what's happening?" he asked, sauntering into Julie's office and pulling a chair around to straddle it backward. He was wearing a T-shirt with the picture of a bloody dagger and a violent message across its front.

Julie suppressed a sigh as she put down the tax report she had been struggling to make sense of. Luis's company was the last thing she needed.

"Hi. I'm pretty busy right now. Could we talk later?"

Luis got up and circled the desk to peer over her shoulder. "Whoa. What's so important that you can't give me a few minutes of your *precious* time?"

He smelled of beer and stale cigarette smoke. Without thinking, she scooted her chair away from him.

"I'm trying to make some sense out of this tax form."

Luis studied Julie's face boldly as he shifted the toothpick in his mouth from one side to the other.

"I don't think you like me."

"That's not true," Julie protested automatically.

Luis brought his face down to hers, and she leaned back. "Prove it." He was too close, and she tried to move again, but he grabbed the arms of her chair with his beefy hands. Julie's eyes grew wide as she stared up at him, trapped. His grin lacked warmth, and his eyes were hard and dangerous. All of a sudden she was afraid.

"Stop it." She wanted to sound firm and cool, but her voice came out high and thin. Next door the phone rang, and overhead the sound of children's feet echoed against the bare floor. She was not alone. If she had to, she could call out and someone would come.

"What's going on?"

Luis straightened immediately, frowning at Connie, who stood in the doorway wearing a suspicious expression.

"Nothin' is going on, buttinski, but it wasn't my idea," Luis said, laughing as he walked to the door, brushing past Connie. "Miss High-and-Mighty here is too good for me." He turned and his gaze locked with Julie's. "You're not too good for Angel, though, are you? 'Cept maybe now he's too good for you."

He took the toothpick out of his mouth and tossed it in the direction of the wastebasket. "Angel will do anything for me. You should both treat me nicer." With a last insulting glance that raked down Connie's lush figure, he turned and walked down the hall, whistling between his teeth.

"What a repulsive man," Connie said as soon as Luis was out of hearing. "Has he bothered you like this before?"

Julie took a deep breath, glad he was gone. "Thanks for coming in when you did. I never know if he's serious." She saw that her hands were trembling, and she clasped them together in her lap. "Does he bother you, too?"

Connie rolled her eyes. "He stares. And I don't mean that he's memorizing my face," she said with a rueful smile. "I think he's trying to mentally figure out my measurements."

Julie returned her friend's smile, feeling a little better. "Lucky us," she said dryly. "All that attention."

Connie shrugged. "I guess he's harmless, but I wish he'd find a job somewhere else."

"Me, too. I don't think he cares about the center or about Angel." Who doesn't deserve a brother like Luis, she thought to herself. It isn't fair.

Connie's phone rang. "Don't let Luis get to you," she said, then went back to her office. Julie returned her attention to the tax form, but it didn't make any more sense than it had earlier. Perhaps her father could explain while she was over there that evening.

She showed it to him after dinner while her mother was talking to Ginny about a luncheon she was hosting the next day. "This is fairly simple," he said. "Here, let me show you what they want."

Julie sat down next to him on the velvet sofa while he explained. In a few moments she understood.

"You make it so easy," Julie said in wonderment. "I must have stared at this for an hour."

"Any more problems I can help you with?"

She folded up the form and put it into her purse. "Not unless you could find a job for Angel's brother," she said without thinking.

"I thought he was working at the center," her mother said, smoothing her linen skirt and sitting down across from them.

Julie sighed. "That's the problem. Whenever Angel isn't there, Luis spends his time talking to me or to Connie. He makes us both nervous."

"He hasn't come on to you, has he?"

Julie's eyebrows rose as she stared at her mother. "Come on to me?" she echoed in a teasing voice.

"I'm not a fossil," her mother said defensively. "I know how to word things."

"Never mind all that." Julie's father leaned forward on the sofa. "*Is* he bothering you?"

"Don't worry," Julie hastened to reassure them both. "It's nothing that I can't handle, and even if I couldn't I know that Angel would set Luis straight." She wished she were as confident as she sounded. Angel had to be told about Luis, and it looked like she was the only one willing to do it.

A worried frown puckered her father's face, then his features relaxed into a rueful smile. "Sometimes I forget that you're grown up," he said quietly. "But I know that you'll be able to take care of whatever's necessary."

"Thanks," Julie said, hoping he was right.

* * *

She watched anxiously for Angel's reaction to what she had told him as he paced the length of his office, deep in thought. His thick brows were pulled together into a thunderous frown, and his mouth was a grim line. Only his eyes were alive with emotion.

For a long moment, as his glittering gaze held hers, Julie wished she'd kept her problems with Luis to herself. She had just finished a garbled explanation, realizing as she talked how vague her complaints must sound.

"Let me understand this," he said, wrenching a hand from his pocket to yank at the knot of his expensive silk tie. "Luis hasn't really said anything insulting or threatening. He hasn't touched you in any way, he hasn't asked you out, but he makes you nervous."

Julie pleated the fabric of her skirt. "Put like that—"

"That's the way you put it to me," he interrupted, throwing his hands up in disgust. "What am I supposed to think, Julie? I asked you to welcome Luis, to make him feel at home at the center. Now you come to me with these accusations. It sounds to me like you're being oversensitive."

His voice softened abruptly. "I know you must have scars from Brad," he said gently, "but all men aren't like that. Granted, Luis had hardly been to a finishing school these last years. He has to learn to get along all over again, especially with women. I had really hoped you could make allowances, let him get to know you, to feel at ease around you."

"I've tried," she burst out. She was starting to feel guilty, until she remembered the way Luis looked at her and the knowing tone to his voice when he made some coarse remark.

She could see mingled pain and frustration in Angel's expression. Only the dawning realization that he wasn't taking her seriously kept her from backing down.

"Maybe you need to try harder," Angel said quietly.

Anger at his unfairness began to seep past the regret she felt in hurting him. Her cheeks heated and her hands curled into fists as frustration replaced sympathy. Obviously he wasn't going to do a damn thing about it.

"I'm sorry," she said stonily, rising. "I should have known better."

Angel almost called her back, then watched silently as she stalked out of his office, her back rigid with temper. The soft click as she shut the door behind her echoed like a pistol shot in the sudden quiet of the room.

"Damn!" Angel picked up the telephone book and threw it against the wall. It hit with a satisfying splat and slid down the wall to land in a wrinkled heap. His first impulse, when she had told him that Luis was making her nervous, had been to find his brother and shake him until his eyes were crossed. No one bothered Julianna, not while Angel was around to prevent it. He had been away when he could have helped her before, and he didn't intend to fail her again.

As she continued to talk, however, stumbling over her words, twisting her hands together anxiously, he had slowly realized that she had no specific complaint. Luis had been away plenty long enough to forget how to act around respectable women, and apparently his taste in jokes was earthier than Julie's. When he had the chance, Angel would remind him to keep it clean. There wasn't much else Angel could do.

Angel bent to retrieve the phone book from the floor, remembering how close he and Luis had been before his brother had been sent away. Once, when Luis was six-teen and Angel was eight, some bigger boys were pick-ing on Angel, taunting him about his blue eyes. Luis had driven up with two buddies, seen the group of boys, and run them all off with threats of beating them to a pulp, either one at a time or all at once.

After that, no one had bothered Angel for a long time, and that evening after Luis's friends had left, he had taken Angel to a show and bought him popcorn. How proud Angel had been to have such a macho brother!

Now he wondered if the reason Julie didn't like Luis was because he was a con, or because he was a full-blooded Mexican. It was an unpleasant thought, one he really didn't want to deal with. She seemed to get along with everyone else, but maybe Angel had been seeing what he wanted to see. Rubbing his aching temples, Angel decided to put the problem aside, hoping that she and Luis could work out their problems without fur-ther difficulties. Angel had enough on his mind with-out playing referee.

Chapter Eight

Over the next couple of days Julie made no attempt to hide her annoyance from Angel. She stayed in her office, ate lunch at her desk instead of joining the others at the large table in the kitchen, and generally went out of her way to avoid him.

She hated the idea of his leaving for New York with the icy wall still between them, but didn't see how she could forget their conversation about Luis. Angel had chosen sides without really listening. Julie had thought they were growing closer lately, and now she felt betrayed by his attitude.

Still, she regretted the wide gulf between them, and she missed Angel's frequent visits to her office when he would perch on the corner of her desk and share with her the latest news about the center, while she drowned in his blue eyes and drank in the mingled scents of his expensive cologne and uniquely sexy aroma.

To keep herself from weakening, she kept her door closed and her nose buried in work. And she found it almost impossible to be civil to Luis. If it hadn't been for his questionable attention, none of this would have happened.

She was barricaded behind her door as usual one morning when Connie began to shriek.

"Angel, Julie, come quick!" Julie could hear the sound of Connie's high-heeled shoes as the other woman raced into Angel's office, leaving a stream of rapid Spanish in her wake.

Julie jumped up and followed her, expecting the worst. An eviction notice, a revoked permit? What could be bad enough to set Connie off?

When Julie skidded to a stop in Angel's doorway, Connie was still shrieking in Spanish and waving a piece of paper.

"What happened? What's the matter?" Julie demanded.

Angel and Luis had been sorting through cartons of donated magazines that were stacked on the floor and across his desk. Angel tried to grab the paper from Connie's hand but failed. Finally he imprisoned her wrist, speaking to her in a firm voice.

"Connie! Speak English! Tell us what's happened."

Julie glanced at Luis. No doubt he understood what Connie had been saying, but other than a narrowing of his dark eyes, he remained motionless.

"*Perdone me!* It's a check from that group Angel spoke to in Seattle. A *grande* check!" Connie's cheeks were flushed, and her hand still fluttered, despite Angel's grip on her wrist.

"The Evergreen Women's Group?" Angel asked, grabbing the paper with his free hand. "Let's see."

His brows shot up and his mouth curved upward in a wide grin. "Hot tamales! Julie, come and look at this!"

She studied the amount written on the check, shocked. "I didn't expect anything like this." As the reality of it sank in, she grinned up at Angel, who exchanged high fives with Luis and gave Connie a hug with the hand holding the check. Before Julie could react further, he grasped her around the waist and swung her in a circle.

"It must have been your charm that impressed them," he said jubilantly, beaming at her. "That's why they were so generous."

She shook her head in denial as he continued to hold her so that her feet didn't touch the floor, her hands resting on his strong shoulders. "No, it was your talk that did it."

Being so close to him was sweet torture. Angel's hands were hot at her waist as he continued to smile. For a moment Julie thought he was going to kiss her right in front of the others.

Then she glimpsed Luis's knowing sneer and began to struggle self-consciously, her mood broken. Embarrassed by the open adoration she was sure that both men must have seen on her face, she backed away.

"That's terrific," she said. "But I have a lot to do. I'll see you later."

Behind her, Angel's excitement turned to puzzlement. Fleetingly he had thought the rift between them might be mended by their pleasure in the unexpected donation, but apparently Julie wasn't as willing to forgive and forget as he was.

It was early the next morning when Angel jumped into his car and turned the key in the ignition. He wanted to get to the center early; he had a full day ahead of him. As the engine roared to life, he glanced up at the gas gauge and cursed. Perhaps the Ferrari needed a tune-up. It sure had been sucking fuel lately. Not for the first time in the last couple of weeks the gauge was lower than he remembered.

He shot around the road's lazy curves and roared through the country club's open gates. At the base of the hill he pulled onto the main road and floored the accelerator, slowing moments later to get gas. It was a glorious morning, the sky so blue it looked artificial, the slight breeze already turning warm. The only dark cloud was the trip ahead of him. New York used to excite him, but now it was only a place, a crowded place without Julie. Too bad he couldn't take her with him. Despite her recent standoffishness, he was sure that New York would bowl her over, just as it had him the first time he saw it.

A lazy smile bent the corners of his mouth. Perhaps if he told her it was for the center... He only wished she were as dedicated to his needs as she was to *Casa del Sol*'s. The idea of Julie tending to his wants was enough to make him shift uncomfortably, as the fit of his jeans became suddenly confining. Perhaps over the week he was away she would find that she missed him as much as he was going to miss her.

Turning his attention to the gas he was pumping into the car, he cursed softly at the lack of discipline that had allowed his thoughts to wander in such a dangerous direction. So far the past still lay between them, but soon they would have to lay it to rest once and for all. Until they did there was no future for them, and he wanted Julie in his future, in his arms and his bed, curled around him....

As he cursed again, the gas pump clunked to a stop. Pulling out his wallet, willing control back to his rampantly responsive body, he crossed to the small office where the attendant was waiting to collect his money. Vaguely he noticed that she gave him an especially warm smile, one he responded to automatically without really seeing her.

Stuffing his change back into his wallet, he returned to the car. On top of its gas guzzling, it needed to be washed. Briefly he considered asking Luis to do it while he was away, then decided it would be less hassle to have Joey take care of it.

More and more he avoided confrontations with Luis, who took little interest in the center and didn't even attend the Hispanic mass at the church in Mount Vernon. Instead he slept most of the day, then watched television and drank beer far into the night after Angel had gone to bed.

"Get off my back," Luis had growled one evening when Angel mentioned that registration for the new quarter at the community college was approaching.

They had been sitting in the rec room having a beer. A thin cigar smoldered between Luis's teeth, and his chin was a forest of black stubble, his expanding gut quivering beneath a new mesh shirt Angel had bought for him along with a closetful of other clothes. "I had all the rehabilitation I could stomach in the joint, little bro. I don't need it from you."

Now Angel slowed the car at the outskirts of town, returning the waves of two high school girls in short skirts who dissolved into giggles when he noticed them. He remembered how close he and Luis had been once. For the first time he allowed himself to wonder if they ever would be again.

Probably the one who appreciated Luis's absence at the center the most was Julie. She hadn't mentioned him again. Still, Luis was turning into a beer-swilling bum. Giving him time to adjust was one thing, supporting his bad habits was another matter entirely, and Angel wished, not for the first time, that Luis would try to meet him halfway.

Angel was leaving for New York the next morning. Julie could hear him talking to Connie about the things that had to be done while he was away, and for the moment she allowed herself to enjoy the blend of gentleness and power in his deep voice. When they were young, the hotter his temper had blazed, the slower his drawl became. He had never threatened, he had promised. When he got angry, his face went expressionless and his eyes iced over. A cold stare and a softly drawled command from Angel made the toughest boys think twice. The few times that hadn't been enough, the wiry power behind his fists solved whatever problem challenged him.

With Julie his voice had gone deep and soft when the need between them was ignited by a look or a touch or a kiss. She shivered with the memory of his young man's passion. He'd kept his hunger tightly leashed until the day that Julie herself turned it loose, the day Angel told her he was leaving Clarkson, the day she chose to use her last and greatest weapon.

The fullest measure of their love had been everything Julie had ever imagined it could be and more, but even then it hadn't been enough to keep him at her side. Brad had never touched that secret part of her that Angel had taken for his own, hadn't even known of its existence. Or apparently cared.

Sometimes Julie wondered how many hotter, more knowing women had shared Angel's bed over the years. He was too physical, too passionate, too devastatingly handsome not to have accepted what surely must have been offered. The thought of him with another woman twisted Julie's insides into a knot of jealous anguish.

Earlier that afternoon he'd asked her to stick around so he could talk to her. His voice had been cool, not surprising after she had retreated from his office so rudely. She hadn't meant to insult him, but only to escape his suffocating nearness and Luis's knowing smirk.

"*Vaya con Dios.* Don't forget where home is." Connie's voice drifted through the open doorway. Julie braced herself and tried to concentrate on the papers spread out before her on the desk.

A sudden change in the atmosphere of her office alerted her to Angel's presence, but she didn't look up right away. Instead she frowned at the letter in her hand until the words merged into a tangle of squiggly black lines. For a moment she got a glimpse of how words and letters must look to a person who couldn't read, but finally she couldn't resist Angel's compelling presence any longer. Slowly she raised her eyes.

He was leaning against the doorjamb, his casual stance a reminder of the poster Julie had tacked up on the back of her bedroom door. His jeans were tight, but this time his chest wasn't bared. Instead he wore a red shirt, half-unbuttoned against the day's muggy heat.

With a mind of its own, her gaze drifted down the tantalizing length of his thighs, their hard power sheathed in soft denim. Angel straightened and moved closer. Flushing, Julie wrenched her attention away from his smoothly flexing muscles as a helpless response to his maleness scorched her cheeks.

She looked up to find him watching her. Slowly, carelessly, his gaze wandered over her body above the desktop, lingering on her breasts. Her nipples were hard, and awareness crackled like static electricity in the silent room.

"I'm leaving," Connie said, pausing in the hallway. "*Adios*, Angel. Julie, see you tomorrow."

"Uh, yes. Tomorrow." Julie took the opportunity to gulp in a deep breath as Angel's attention was diverted. The intrusion had shattered the tension in the room, and she was determined not to let it build again.

"So what did you want to see me about?" she asked when he shut the door and swung around to face her.

An unreadable expression flickered across his face before his thick lashes came down to shutter his eyes. He ignored the straight-backed chair, sitting instead on the corner of her desk as usual. Julie braced herself to keep from rolling her chair back. Her reaction to him was getting harder to control.

"You coming back this evening?"

"Yes, after I eat. I'm meeting with some of the tutors later, then filling in for Ray. His wife is sick, and he asked me to take over for him tonight. I like to work with the students, they're so eager to learn."

"True. Let's get something to eat while I make sure we've covered everything for when I'm gone. I have to be back here later myself. The owner of the cheese-processing plant wants a tour before he agrees to a corporate sponsorship." His tone was professional, but his narrowed eyes offered a challenge she couldn't resist.

Julie hesitated for a split second, then nodded. "Thank you."

"Pizza okay? There's a new place out toward Anacortes. We'll be back in plenty of time for your class."

While they ate Angel kept the conversation on work, bringing Julie up to date on the corporate sponsors he was wooing and other new sources of revenue he was exploring. Besides that, he was the assistant coach on one of the boys' baseball teams, and he bragged about their enthusiasm.

"If there's an emergency, Joey knows where to reach me in New York," he said as they pulled back into the parking lot. "If you think of anything else, I'll be around until we lock up this evening."

"Don't you have to pack?"

He looked down at her as they walked up the steps. "I travel light."

For a moment, bitter memories assailed her. "How could I forget," she said before she went through the door. Then she turned, almost colliding with him. "Thanks for the pizza."

"No problem." His fingers closed around her upper arm. "Someday you and I are going to have a talk."

"I thought that's what we were just doing."

Displeasure tightened his bronzed face. "That's not what I meant. We can't go on like this forever."

Apprehensive, Julie walked away without responding, locking her purse in a desk drawer before going to one of the bigger rooms to pull the chairs into a circle. What was the point in reliving the past? It was done and they couldn't go back, even if one of them was crazy enough to want to.

Two hours later she was finished. She switched on the light in her office and sat down to retrieve her purse, hoping to leave before she ran into Angel again. She was tired, her defenses were down, and the building was silent. Everyone else had probably already left.

As she pushed shut the desk drawer, Angel came into the room and stopped, studying her with a shuttered gaze. "You aren't afraid of me, are you?"

His question surprised her. "No, of course not."

Without taking his eyes from hers, he moved around the desk to where she was sitting. As Julie watched him, his warm hands closed over her shoulders, urging her up.

"Why did you pull away from me the other day?"

He was standing too close, and the directness of his question surprised her. It was the last thing she expected him to ask. Their bodies were almost touching, but when she tried to step back, his hands held her still.

"Why, Julie?"

It was difficult to explain without confessing her reaction to him, or trying to explain the way Luis's stare had made her feel. The last thing she wanted to do was to criticize Luis again. Without a qualm, Julie took the coward's way out.

"I don't know what you mean."

His eyes darkened, and a muscle twitched in his lean cheek. "When I swung you around," he prompted. "I thought afterward that I might have frightened you."

"Oh, that. I just had a lot of work to finish."

His gaze probed hers, and then he sighed, releasing his grip on her shoulders. "I'll accept that for now."

She expected him to turn away, or to begin discussing something about her duties while he was gone, even though they had been over everything already. Instead he lifted his hand and laid it against her cheek.

"I wouldn't hurt you," he murmured.

A tremble went through her as his knuckles trailed along her jaw. "I know that." When her lips parted, his thumb brushed against them. He swallowed and leaned closer, his aura reaching out to enfold her.

Julie's mouth was dry, and she could feel her heart hammering in her breast, but she didn't move away. No power on earth could have made her retreat from what she saw blazing in Angel's eyes.

Desire burned there, as it burned deep within her. With an almost soundless murmur, he tipped her head back as her hands cupped his elbows and slid up his arms.

"Querida," he sighed as his mouth covered hers.

The dam of Julie's resistance broke with a rush and she returned his kiss, her lips pressing against his then parting for the welcome thrust of his tongue. Angel's arms went around her as she locked hers about his neck. Her feminine curves meshed with the hard angles of his body. His hand buried itself in her hair, holding her head still for the blistering heat of his mouth.

He explored her lips and the dark warmth beyond with greedy thoroughness, finally breaking away to string kisses across her closed eyes and down her jaw. Trembling wildly, Julie arched her neck to give him better access to the sensitive spot below her ear. Her hands stroked his throat, then slid inside his collar.

Angel groaned, finding her lips again, this kiss rougher, hotter, as Julie stayed with him, her tongue stroking his, her fingers dancing across his chest.

Angel nudged her with his hips, his arousal butting against her welcoming warmth. Julie tilted her head back as he nipped at her neck, then soothed the spot with his tongue. As she arched away, her lower body pressed even closer. Angel swore under his breath as his hands locked on her hips, holding her tight against him. Fire raced through Julie's body, and her mind clouded as Angel backed her against the wall, sliding one hard thigh between her knees.

"I want you," he groaned, his voice a sensual rasp. "I ache for you." He captured her hand in his, and rubbed it against the swell beneath his jeans. "Feel how much I want you."

Julie's hand curled against the power of his need. She was burning up.

Her hand slid across his thigh to linger on the outside of his hip as Angel gently rocked against her. He threw back his head, eyes tightly shut, and a long breath hissed between his clenched teeth.

"God, baby, you feel so good."

His words inflamed her. "So do you. Oh, Angel, so do you." The feelings he was arousing tangled together with her memories as passion claimed her. She clung to him even harder as he thrust his body tantalizingly against her.

For a moment they clung together, both gasping for breath as a hard shudder tore through Angel. Julie gloried in her power to arouse him to such a fever pitch, even as her knees threatened to buckle.

Footsteps down the hallway and the banging of the front door rolled back the white-hot madness of desire, reminding Julie where they were. The front door was unlocked and her sparse office was hardly the place for what she and Angel were hurtling toward with terrifying speed.

She dropped her arms, and before Angel could protest, she slid away so that their overheated bodies were no longer touching. Angel's arm loosed its grip as he slumped and gritted his teeth.

"Ever since I returned I've wanted you naked and hungry," he said, head bowed and voice thick with unsatisfied lust. "I wish to hell I wasn't leaving now. You'll rebuild the wall, and I'll have to start all over again to tear it down."

What could Julie say to that? She wanted—no, needed time to repair her defenses. Her hands were shaking as she leaned around him to pick up her purse.

"I don't know what you mean."

"The hell you don't." His face was a portrait of frustration. "The passion between us is still there. Denying it won't make it go away."

Julie didn't look to see if he was coming as she switched off the light and stepped into the hallway. He was right. Her response to him had exploded like a flash fire, hot and compelling. Whatever reservations she might hold, she still wanted him with burning intensity.

Her hand shook as she reached for the heavy front door. He was so close behind her that she could hear him breathing.

"Wait a minute while I set the alarm. Then I'll follow you home."

"That's not necessary," she protested, panicking.

"It's late. Remember that you don't live in the best neighborhood anymore." His face was set in stubborn lines.

She knew it was pointless to argue. With an exasperated sigh, she walked to her car, gazing up at the starry night. Resisting the childish urge to try to outrun him, she waited until he'd started his engine and signaled, then drove slowly down the bumpy road. As she stared at the path her headlights cut into the darkness, memories of her one afternoon of love with Angel before he went away filled her heart.

He had been a wonderful lover—ardent, tender, patient. Even when Julie sensed that his control must be at the breaking point he had held back, putting her needs ahead of his own. Her pain was minimal as they became one for the first time, followed by a flood of sweet passion she hadn't dreamed was possible. He had thought to take care of her, too, admitting that he carried protection in case his resolve toward her ever weakened.

Afterward Angel had cradled her tenderly, murmuring love words, making her feel beautiful and precious. Remembering how perfect it had been was not the best way to strengthen her resolve now. As she pulled up in front of her apartment, Julie admitted to herself that, for tonight, the last thing she wanted was to go through that front door alone.

When Angel parked his car behind hers instead of driving on, she almost sighed with relief, and as she waited on the front porch for him it seemed like she had been waiting forever. He took the steps two at a time and slid his arm around her waist, their eyes meeting in wordless communication. Glorying in the heat from his passionate gaze, Julie couldn't dredge up a single reason to refuse him, couldn't even seem to think. All she had to say was no. Instead she unlocked the door and held it open wide.

Angel's eyes were black in the night's dimness, and his face was somber. "Are you sure?" His voice was deep and heavy with desire.

Speech was almost impossible, as mingled fear and longing choked her. "I'm sure," she finally whispered.

As he followed her inside, she reached for the light switch, but his hand clamped on her wrist.

"We have the moonlight," he said. His fingers skimmed lightly down her cheek, his touch igniting a fiery trail as he explored the rim of her ear, then traced the shape of her collarbone, making her tremble.

Later she would have the time to rebuild those walls, Julie told herself. To sort out the blame that lay between them. Tonight belonged to memories and to love. Tonight belonged to two high school sweethearts who had never had a chance. Just this once she meant to take what Angel was offering. Just this once she wanted to feel like the woman he had made her into.

He took her hand in his, touching his lips to her palm. Then he ran his tongue over the sensitive skin before lacing his fingers through hers. Wordlessly she led him through the darkened living room. In her open bedroom doorway he stopped, lifting her hair aside to place a light kiss on the curve of her neck. Julie lifted a hand to caress his shoulder, a sigh breaking from her lips.

Behind her, Angel was fighting for the control to make the night beautiful for them both. His need was almost overwhelming. Never had he wanted anyone like he wanted Julie now, and only iron determination kept him from letting his passion consume them.

He didn't question why she had allowed him inside or what she was thinking. He only cared about the love they were rekindling with each kiss, each touch. He knew now that there had never been anyone for him but Julie, that there never would be again. Somehow he had to show her that they belonged together, and for that he needed the strength and the patience to love her the way she deserved to be loved, slowly and thoroughly.

She slipped away from him, dropping her purse and turning to switch the bedside lamp on low. "Angel—" Her voice was like sunshine in the dim glow of the room. The light shone against the brass headboard and shimmered in her hair.

"Shhh, my love. We'll talk later. For now..." He let his hands tell her what he wanted, drawing her into his embrace. Again passion flared between them. Angel pressed a hungry kiss on her mouth, then his fingers went to the buttons of her V-necked shirt.

"You're even more beautiful than I remembered," he said as he freed the first two buttons. His head bowed and he touched his lips to the white skin above her lacy bra. Julie gasped, and the blood pounded through him with savage intensity, pooling hotly, heavily, until his need was a physical ache. Ignoring the discomfort, he released the next button and spread her collar wide. A floral scent, mixed with Julie's own intoxicating fragrance, rose to fill his nostrils as her hands clutched his waist.

He turned her slightly so the dim glow from the lamp bathed her face. Her eyes were wide as she watched him, her mouth slightly swollen from the kisses he'd already pressed against it.

"Touch me," he urged. "I'm on fire for you."

With a little sigh, she lightly stroked the skin exposed by his partly unbuttoned shirt. It wasn't enough, and with an impatient gesture Angel wrenched the shirt open the rest of the way. A button bounced against the floor with a tiny ping.

"Touch me," he said again.

Blood roared in Julie's ears as she laid her hands against his hot skin, absorbing the thunderous beating of his heart below the silver medal he always wore. One thumb scraped against a small male nipple, and he groaned deep in his throat, trembling wildly. She bent her head in a bold caress and touched her lips to the tiny bump, drawing a hiss of reaction.

Quickly his fingers dealt with the rest of the buttons on her blouse. When he slid the soft fabric over her shoulders and down her arms, his knuckles left a fiery trail that his seeking mouth followed. The blouse dropped to the floor and he lifted her arm, dragging his tongue across the sensitive skin of her inner elbow. Julie tugged at the fabric of his shirt and he shrugged out of it. His hand circled behind her and the bra's catch gave way. Julie held it to her as he drew the straps slowly down her arms. Angel's face was taut with passionate intensity, and when she let the bra fall away, he examined her bared breasts in lengthy silence.

"They're as beautiful as I remembered." His voice was reverent, and Julie flushed with pride.

His hands lifted the rounded fullness as he bent his head to draw one hardened tip into his mouth. His fingers caressed the other.

Julie swayed against him, her knees gone to jelly. When her hands touched his bare back, the fire gathering in her belly burned hotter. The rhythmic pull of his lips on her nipple turned the flames into a roaring inferno.

She speared her fingers through his hair, holding his bowed head tight against her. The hand that had been shaping her other breast skimmed down to explore the waistband of her skirt. As Julie nipped at his ear, Angel raised his head and kissed her deeply as his nimble fingers found the button and zipper in the back of the skirt and released them. He bent, pulling skirt and slip down with him as she kicked off her sandals.

It had been a warm day and the only other garment Julie wore was high-cut panties. Angel sank to the floor, his mouth starting at her knees and working its way back upward with maddening slowness. When he reached the top of her thighs, a tremor ripped through Julie. His thumbs hooked the narrow waistband and he slid it downward, tracing the path with his mouth. His heated breath fanned against the skin of her stomach, his hands sliding around to cup her buttocks as he eased her down onto the bed.

Julie's mind turned to fire, and her body to liquid heat as he straightened, caressing her with his eyes. Her bones were water, and she lay back without protest as Angel stripped off his jeans and boots. When he joined her on the bed, only dark knit briefs separated their heated flesh. Her hands fluttered over his hair to his neck and across his bare chest as he watched her.

Julie rolled to her side and ran a hand over his narrow hip, scraping her nails against the bone. Angel trembled violently at her touch, shifting onto his back. Mimicking his earlier movements, she slipped the tips of her fingers into his elastic waistband. His breath froze in his throat as she delved deeper. Wiry hair brushed the backs of her knuckles as her fingers investigated.

Angel groaned, sweat breaking out on his forehead as he fought to keep from rolling over and pinning her to the bed. Her questing fingers were tearing his good intentions to shreds.

Julie withdrew her hand and tugged lightly at his briefs, inching the garment down his legs. With a heartfelt curse, Angel lifted his hips and yanked them off. "*Now* touch me," he challenged.

To his utter amazement she did. Her fingers curled around him possessively, and Angel's control shattered like fine crystal. His fingers clamped around her wrist.

"No!"

His denial made her freeze. What had she done wrong? For a moment uncertainty shoved desire aside.

"What's the matter?" Her voice seemed to come from somewhere else.

Instantly his arms swept around her as he pushed her to her back and covered her body with his. "Nothing, my sweet love. Nothing but hunger that is driving me crazy and your touch that sends me over the edge."

He lowered his head, kissing her deeply, and the need she felt for him came flooding back. She arched, rubbing against his heated flesh.

"Angel!" she cried.

He slid a muscular thigh between her trembling legs. "Open for me," he rasped.

Julie could deny him nothing. Her head was swimming as he lifted her higher. Then with one long gliding stroke, he buried himself to the hilt in her wet warmth.

For a moment he lay still, and she savored the feel of him deep within her. Then as if he could wait no longer, he began to move. Julie rose to meet each powerful thrust, her nails digging into his back as his breath hissed against her ear. She wanted it to last forever, but already her body was beginning to pulsate around him. Her tremors and helpless little cries triggered Angel's release. The force of his passion ripped through them both, and groaning her name, he gave himself up to her.

For long moments Julie lay within his embrace, as she slowly drifted back to earth. Her body ached pleasantly, and she felt as if her very bones had dissolved in the heat of their lovemaking. Beside her, Angel flopped to his back, one arm anchoring her close to his side.

He cradled her to him as he took in long gulps of air. "You're so wonderful," he said, his hands sweeping down her sides and around to cup her rounded bottom before teasing back up her spine. "I was like a boy with you, a gun ready to misfire."

"I'm sorry," she murmured. "I didn't mean to—"

His laugh cut her off. "God, don't be sorry. I've dreamed of this. Let me savor it."

He gathered her close and Julie could sense the desire building in him once more. Her own senses were reawakening too, the intensity surprising her. Moments before she had been completely satisfied, replete. Now she was starving for him, as if she hadn't just crested a peak she didn't know could be so high.

She trembled as Angel rose over her, bending to tease first one breast and then the other with his mouth, lashing with his tongue and tugging gently with his lips. She reached for him but he shook his head.

"Let me," he murmured. "Just relax."

His request was impossible to follow as his insistent mouth and tongue explored every swell and hollow. His fingers skimmed down her ribs and investigated the sensitive skin beneath her breasts as his tongue dipped into her navel, then tickled the downy line that bisected her stomach. As his fingers caressed her intimately, starting new fires blazing deep within her, his mouth returned to hers, kissing her deeply, probing with his tongue till she drew it inside her mouth and stroked it with her own.

Angel broke the kiss and burrowed his head against her neck. "I usually have more control, but it's been so long, and you're so warm, so giving."

She thought about his words as he held her, wondering if it really had been a long time for him or if he was just saying that.

He must have sensed her thoughts because he paused, looking deep into her eyes. "It's been since way before I decided to come back here," he said quietly. "I knew then that everything else was a pale imitation of what we had. Even when I thought you were married I couldn't make myself want anyone else. Not really."

"It was the same for me," she whispered. "Brad never, I never, I mean he couldn't . . ."

Angel propped himself up on one elbow. "You didn't enjoy it with him?"

She shook her head, embarrassed. "I haven't since that first time with you."

His eyes widened. "There's been no one else?"

"No one."

"I'm glad," he said as he bent to kiss her. Soon Julie was spinning away again, a helpless victim of the passion that exploded between them. If anything, the final eruption was even more intense than the one before. After it was over, Julie could barely move. Angel collapsed against her for a long moment before shifting to her side. They shared a pillow, and she could feel the intensity of his gaze.

"Now I know what beds were made for," he gasped finally.

Her laugh was wry. "I'm sure you discovered that long ago," she said, trying to keep the jealousy from her voice. She had barely recovered from the tempestuous moments they had shared, and he was already reminding her that he had a past separate from hers.

Angel rolled onto one elbow and stared down at her. "I want you to know something," he said in a serious voice. "Nothing, nowhere, was ever remotely like what you and I just shared."

When Julie didn't answer, he sat up and grabbed her chin in his fingers, forcing her to look at him. Julie stared into the intense blue of his eyes.

"I mean it," he said. "Sex is one thing, but it doesn't touch what we have together. *Making love* with you is beyond anything I've ever experienced."

Julie's gaze shifted away as happiness at his words flooded through her. Her emotions were in turmoil, her defenses had been shattered. Beside her, Angel jammed the extra pillow behind his back. Feeling at a disadvantage, Julie did the same.

"Interesting decor," he said, pointing at the closed bedroom door.

Oh, Lord, the poster! She had never dreamed he would ever be in her bedroom when she had hung it there. "You know how it is," she said with an embarrassed grin and what she hoped came across as a casual shrug, "when you have to fill up the blank spaces."

Angel studied her intently for a long moment. "So?" he finally asked.

"So, what?"

"How do you feel about me now?"

Chapter Nine

Wordlessly Julie looked at Angel, her emotions in a turmoil. How could she tell him how she felt when she wasn't sure herself? Too much had happened in her life for her to be able to blurt out what was in her heart. As he continued to wait, she tried to formulate some answer that would satisfy him, but the caution she had learned so painfully rose in her throat to block out the words.

Angel hadn't said he loved her. What if all he felt was desire? And now he had satisfied it. What if, even worse, he had wanted to exact some kind of revenge because he still thought she had betrayed him? She tried to read the expression in his eyes but couldn't. It wouldn't be the first time she had misjudged a man's intentions, a man she thought cared for her.

"Still the same old Julie," Angel said after long moments had passed. He was obviously upset by her hesitation. "Weighing all the options, aren't you?" When he slid from her bed, the sight of his rangy form was almost enough to distract her from his angry words.

"What do you mean?" She yanked the sheet over her exposed breasts, suddenly shy before his look of glaring disapproval.

Angel scooped up his clothes, glancing at the clock radio on her nightstand. "I thought I might have changed enough to make a difference, but I was wrong, wasn't I? You're still not about to take a chance with the half-breed bastard from the wrong end of town."

His bitter words shocked Julie speechless. As he turned his back to pull on his briefs and jeans, she slid from the opposite side of the bed, wrapping a pink seersucker robe quickly around her.

"I never felt that way!"

He glanced over one wide shoulder, eyes cold as ice. The words he uttered shocked her. "I'm not the naive kid I was when I left," he said. "I thought you'd changed, but I was wrong. You still weigh the options before you commit yourself. You still won't trust yourself to me."

His accusation infuriated Julie, who remembered quite clearly how she had felt when Joey told her Angel was gone. "How dare you talk about trust?" she blazed, yanking a knot into the belt of her robe. "You didn't trust me enough to stay here and make a life together, and *you* haven't changed either. You're still pigheaded!"

His hands stilled on the buttons of his shirt. She felt a perverse satisfaction when she saw the dangling thread where one had been ripped loose earlier. "What do you mean?"

"*You* still don't trust *me*!"

"The hell I don't."

"You didn't even believe me when I came to you for help with Luis. You thought I was some hysterical female with an ego problem."

"Luis?" The puzzlement in his eyes fueled her anger. He didn't even remember her complaint!

"I know he's your brother," she cried, "but you'd better wake up. He's nothing like you and he's headed for trouble."

"Leave Luis out of this! You don't like him and you don't trust me. What's your problem? Are you too uptight to make a rational decision about any man whose skin is darker than your own?"

Julie's mouth fell open and she stared. Color spread across Angel's cheeks as he focused all his attention on fastening his belt. Then he sat on the edge of the bed and pulled on his boots while Julie opened and closed her mouth like a fish. Dear God, how could he believe what he had just said?

Sensing his hurt, and battling her own confusion and pain at his unjust accusation, she tried to explain. "I refused to run away with you because I thought we would both be better off staying here in Clarkson," she said, sitting next to him on the bed and touching his arm with a hand that trembled.

Angel's bark of laughter was cruelly sarcastic, making her jerk away from him. "You still think I'm just some dumb Chicano you can fool, don't you? The real reason you backed out was because you didn't want to give up college and all that lovely financial security for the questionable future I could give you. No glamour in being the wife of an army private, huh? You didn't know then that I'd hit it big, did you? Maybe if I had come back after my first win, or my tenth, you would have treated me differently.''

Tears filled Julie's eyes and she leaped up, staring out the window while she brushed them away. ''How could I have treated you any differently? I loved you!'' And I still love you, she thought, turning to gaze at him imploringly.

His disbelieving expression didn't alter.

''You don't understand,'' she said, desperation coloring her voice.

''No, *you* don't understand. How did you feel when you saw my picture in the paper? When you saw me on the cover of some magazine?'' He leaned closer, his face carved from stone. ''Did you regret your decision then, Julianna? Did you?''

Confusion stilled her tongue. How could she convince him that she had regretted her decision every day for ten long years? His accusation rang in her ears. Was he right about her not wanting to give up what she had? Could she have been so wrong about herself, thinking she was sacrificing her happiness when all she really was doing was looking out for her own skin?

Shaken, Julie glanced away, her fingers toying with the ends of her belt. She needed to sort things out, but it was very late and she was so tired. Her brain refused to cooperate.

As she faced him again, Angel raked an impatient hand through his hair. Then he sucked in a deep breath, and the hard expression on his face softened slightly.

''Look,'' he said, ''I shouldn't have lost my temper like that. I know that you were too young and I asked too much of you. In reality, I forgave you long ago. I don't know why I said all those things tonight. It just hurt when you wouldn't be honest with me about what you were feeling.''

Julie couldn't believe her ears. He had the nerve, the unmitigated gall, to stand there with a self-righteous expression on his face and tell her that he *forgave* her? Not only had he completely dismissed his own ten-year silence as well as her unselfishness in putting his needs before her own, but he had the sheer brass to magnanimously forgive her for a crime she hadn't committed.

As she stared at Angel, white-faced, he took her silence as an admission of guilt. Not for a moment did he buy her explanation that she had done it for him. He had wanted her to go; how could her staying behind have been in his interest? She knew nothing of the loneliness he had suffered, the doubts, the terrible pain over his mother's death. He had needed Julie and she hadn't been there.

Instead she had stayed behind at the safe little high school, then gone on to college and Brad. While Angel had been building a life from nothing, Julie had probably been filling hers with football games and sorority teas.

''What's the matter?'' he asked finally, breaking the silence between them. ''Can't you think of another lie to tell me? Perhaps that you missed me while you were dating all the campus Casanovas? Or how much you wished I was there in my faded jeans and black jacket to escort you to the dances?''

His baiting tone brought fresh heat to Julie's cheeks, but she kept her lips firmly closed. What puzzled her the most was that beneath his anger she could have sworn she saw a glimmer of pain. He had forgiven her, he'd said, and had apparently dismissed her a long time before. Earlier that night he had satisfied whatever curiosity he might have had about her performance in bed. So why that shadow of pain?

She was the one who had a right to be hurt, not him.

For a moment he waited as if he still expected her to explain herself. When she still didn't answer, he glanced again at the clock. "I have a plane to catch. I can find the door."

Julie watched his progress through the darkened living room. He bumped against a chair but didn't stop, didn't turn. Instead he wrenched open the front door and descended the steps into the darkness. With tears running down her face, she crossed the room to lock the door behind him before going back into the bedroom.

It was only after he had left that her earlier doubts returned. Perhaps they had both been wrong. "Oh, Angel," she whispered, looking up at his poster, "we'll never find our way back together. What am I to do?"

"Earth to Julie. Is anyone there?"

Julie blinked and focused on Stef's perplexed expression. "I was listening," she said defensively. "You were reminding me how bad the food was at our tenth high school reunion."

Stef rolled her eyes. "Sure I was. Fifteen minutes ago. I've been telling you about the promotions at work, and you haven't heard a word I've said."

Tom was at a weekend seminar in Portland, so Stef had stayed the night with Julie. They'd gone shopping in Seattle on Saturday, and today they were sitting around the apartment talking and sharing the fat Sunday newspaper.

At least Stef was talking, but Julie's mind kept straying to Angel and what had happened between them. She couldn't seem to push him from her thoughts no matter what she did.

"Maybe if you talked about it," Stef suggested. "You might as well. I can't get you to concentrate on anything else."

"Talk about what?"

"Whatever's doing such a heavy-duty number on your head. Even that half-price sale at Nordstrom's yesterday didn't make you smile."

Stef helped herself to an orange from the bowl of fruit on the coffee table. "You're a million miles away." She stopped peeling the orange abruptly and her gaze narrowed. "Or maybe not quite that far. What's the distance between here and New York City, anyway?"

Julie flushed, tucking her bare feet under her. "I have no idea. New York might as well be on the far side of the moon from here. But what difference does it make, anyway?"

Stef was nothing if not persistent. "Why don't you tell me what's wrong?"

"Wrong?" Julie echoed. How could she tell her friend that she'd made love with Angel and it was better than she had remembered, that she knew for certain that she still loved him but was miserable because they were farther apart than ever? "Nothing's wrong. I'm just wondering whether Angel can get enough corporate backing to keep the center open," she improvised.

"Give me a break." Stef slid onto the floor, resting her back against the couch.

"Pardon me?"

"I told you when Angel came back that there was more to it than you thought," Stef said. "Aren't things going well between you?"

Julie looked down at her friend, determined not to discuss Angel with her, and promptly burst into tears.

It was still early when Julie went to bed, knowing she wouldn't sleep but needing the basic creature comfort of burying her head beneath the covers. Stef had finally given up and left to meet Tom at the Sea-Tac airport, but not before she slapped a box of tissues into Julie's hands and told her to call anytime if she wanted to talk.

Only a few minutes passed before Julie kicked the covers impatiently aside. She was wide awake. Perhaps herb tea would help her to feel drowsy—that and the new bestseller with the slow beginning she had been determined to wade through. The summer sounds of children laughing, dogs barking and radios playing filtered through the closed window as she padded to the kitchen.

Julie had barely put the water on to boil when the telephone rang. Glancing at the clock, she turned off the burner under the kettle and reached for the phone.

When she put the receiver to her ear, the first thing she heard was the telltale static of a long-distance call. Her fingers tightened as she cautiously murmured a greeting.

"Julie, it's me. Don't hang up," Angel said quickly.

She was tempted to do just that, despite the way his voice always affected her, but curiosity kept her receiver pressed to her ear. "What do you want?" She realized how unfriendly she must sound, and reminded herself that Angel was her boss. He was probably calling about business.

There was a long pause, and Julie toyed with the phone cord, wishing she could start over.

"Hell," he said finally. "I don't even know why I'm calling. I guess I was just homesick."

Julie snorted disbelievingly. "You?"

"Yeah, me. I think of Clarkson as my home now, and I intend to stay there. Traveling isn't as much fun as it used to be."

"So why didn't you call Luis? Or Juan or Ben?" His reasoning wasn't particularly flattering, and Julie couldn't prevent the resentment from creeping into her voice after the way they had parted company. She hadn't expected him to call her at all.

"Maybe I should have tried one of them. I hope I'm not interrupting anything, but I just wanted to hear a voice from home." There was a pause, and it sounded like he took a drink of something. "I wanted to hear *your* voice," he said more quietly.

"So," he continued before she could think of a reply, "everything okay with you?"

She was feeling guilty for the way she had sounded. "Everything's fine here. How's New York?"

"Hot. Crowded. Noisy."

"Have you started the commercials yet?"

"My agent gave me a script to look over. The real work doesn't begin until tomorrow morning. We'll be doing some shots in Central Park."

"At least you'll be outside."

"True."

There was another long silence. "Well," Angel said, "guess I had better let you go. I didn't wake you, did I?"

"No, it's early here."

"Oh, yeah. I forgot. It's late here, but I couldn't sleep. I'll see you next weekend, or a week from tomorrow, I guess."

"Okay. Good luck with the ad campaign."

"Thanks. Good night."

"Uh, Angel?"

"What?" His voice gentled.

"I'm glad you called."

She could hear his breathing. "Me, too. Maybe I'll call you again if I get the chance."

"That would be nice."

Julie didn't hang up the receiver until she heard the click at the other end, then she slid down into the old chair, her arms wrapped around her bent knees, and savored some of the memories that his voice had rekindled.

They were sitting in the secondhand car Angel had bought and fixed up, watching the sunset. Julie was supposed to be at a movie with Stef, not parked along Chuckanut Drive, snuggled next to Angel while they talked about their future.

"By the time I graduate from college," she said, "you'll have your own garage. We can buy a little house, and I'll teach school. Until the babies come." She could feel her cheeks grow hot at the idea of having Angel's babies.

His fingers toyed with one of the tiny silver-and-turquoise earrings he'd surprised her with earlier that evening. "I thought your folks wanted you to be a lawyer," he said.

Julie shifted sideways on the worn seat, running her hand lightly up his bare arm as she smiled into his face. "But it's not what I want," she said. "Besides, that takes too long. The sooner I graduate, the sooner we can get married and really be together."

If Angel had any doubts about her plans, he kept them to himself. It had become more and more difficult to keep from going all the way in their lovemaking. Julie sensed his growing frustration and sometimes she wished he wouldn't stop, but not even with Angel could she be so forward as to suggest it herself.

She continued to stroke his arm until he caught her wandering hand in his. His gaze was heavy with promise as he bent toward her. "That's a long time we'll have to wait, *querida*, but I will wait as long as it takes."

Three days later Angel's mother was killed, and everything changed forever.

Julie drummed her fingers restlessly. Perhaps he had been right. If she had trusted him and not been so cautious, her life would be very different now. Lord knew she had enough regrets about the path she had chosen. With a grumble of disgust, she turned out the lights and went back to her lonely bedroom, sure she wouldn't sleep a wink.

The next morning it was all she could do to keep her eyes open as she drafted replies to some of the routine correspondence that Angel hadn't had time to deal with before he left.

From the next office, Julie could hear Connie humming a cheerful tune as the file cabinet drawers slid open and slammed back shut with a regularity that set Julie's teeth on edge.

She was digging around in her purse for an aspirin when Connie sailed through the adjoining door, a big smile on her pretty face.

"Isn't it a wonderful morning?" Connie trilled, skirts swirling around her petite figure.

Julie glanced up, then set her purse back on the floor. "Bah, humbug."

"I beg your pardon?"

"Old Anglo-Saxon term. Means I don't agree with your outlook on life."

The confusion cleared from Connie's face. "Rough weekend?"

"No, just didn't sleep well last night. How about you?"

Her offhand question was apparently all the encouragement that Connie needed. She dragged a straight-backed chair closer, sat down and propped her elbow on the desk.

"Joey took me to dinner Friday night, then we spent all day Saturday with my kids. He really liked them." Her dark eyes were sparkling, and her honey-toned cheeks were flushed with color.

Julie realized she'd been so preoccupied with her own problems that she hadn't been paying attention to anything that was going on around her.

"Sounds serious," she said, smiling.

Anxiety clouded Connie's expression with the suddenness of a Pacific Northwest rain shower, and the sparkle faded from her eyes. "Joey's a terrific guy," she said. "But I'm so mixed up."

Concern for her new friend made Julie reach across the desk and pat Connie's arm reassuringly. "Care to tell me about it?" Stef's voice asking her the same thing echoed in Julie's head.

Connie's red-tipped fingers fluttered expressively, but she pressed her lips together and shrugged.

"Are you mixed up because he works for Angel?" Julie probed gently. "Do you wish he did something else?"

Connie's black brows rose in surprise. "Oh, no. It's because of Carlos, my husband." She blinked rapidly, dashing a tear from her lashes with the back of her hand. "When he was killed I thought I'd never love another man, that I'd never find real happiness again. You understand?"

Julie nodded.

"I really loved Carlos. He was the only boy I ever dated, and we married when we were teenagers. I still love him." She began to toy with the string of carved, clay beads around her neck. "It's been over a year now, and the children adore Joey."

Julie rose and came around the desk to touch Connie's shoulder. "I'm sure that Carlos loved you very much," she said slowly, searching for the right words. "And from all you told me about him, he would want you and the kids to be happy. Wouldn't you wish the same for him if you were the one to have been taken away so suddenly, so young?"

Connie thought for a moment, then slowly agreed. "You're right. I would not want Carlos to be alone." She got up and threw her arms around Julie. "*Gracias!* I feel much better now. The guilt...but you have reminded me that Carlos would be happy for me."

"Joey's a good man," Julie added. "I hope that things work out for the two of you."

After Connie left, resuming her cheerful humming, Julie tried to get back to work. Instead she found herself studying with great interest the ballpoint pen she was slowly twirling in her fingers. Stef had Tom, Connie had Joey, and Julie had her memories. Terrific. Her mood plummeted once again and she got up to shut the adjoining door tight, blocking out the renewed sounds of Connie's happiness.

* * *

After that one futile phone call, Angel was glad when everything was wrapped up on schedule and he was able to fly home. He watched impatiently as the plane landed and taxied toward the gate. Soon he would be able to see for himself whether or not Julie had missed him. He had already given up his own battle, planning to go to her as soon as possible.

"Hey, *amigo*, good flight?" Joey asked when Angel came off the plane and they embraced briefly.

"Good enough, I guess. How are you? Where's Luis?" Angel glanced around, but his brother was nowhere in sight.

Joey looked away. "He was busy, said he'd see you at home later."

Angel started walking toward the baggage claim area. "Let's get going," he said over his shoulder. "I want to see Julie."

He dropped Joey back at the house, then went directly to her apartment. It was only early evening in Clarkson, but Angel was still on New York time and it had been a stressful week. He hoped she wasn't still at the center. For the first time he didn't have the energy that the *Casa* demanded of him.

When he turned down her street he was happy to see her car there and a light on in her kitchen. Parking the Ferrari, he killed the motor and slammed the door, taking the steps to her apartment two at a time.

When Julie answered his knock, instinct took over. Angel pulled her into his arms. She clung to him like a child as he buried his face in her hair, inhaling her scent.

"You're back," she said unnecessarily.

"I wish it could have been sooner. How are you?"

"Fine now," she mumbled, still holding on to him.

Angel found himself desperately hoping that she was as glad to see him as her actions indicated. Keeping one arm around her, he eased inside and shut the door behind him.

She pulled away, and he cupped her face between his hands. There were purple shadows beneath her hazel eyes, giving her creamy skin a bruised look. He brushed across it with his thumb.

"Long hours?" he asked gently.

She turned away, indicating that he sit on the couch. "Would you like some coffee?"

"I'd love some if it's made." It took all his control to let her go when he wanted to keep her nestled close to him.

She brought him a steaming mug and sat down across from him. "How was New York?"

He made a dismissive gesture with one hand. "Okay, but how are you, really? You look tired."

Julie was so busy taking in his beloved features and absorbing the fact that he was actually there that she almost missed the question. "What? Oh, I'm fine. It's been busy at work, of course—"

Angel frowned and cut her off. "You know that's not what I meant," he said, his patience obviously gone.

She took a sip of her coffee, stalling for time. She didn't want to reveal how much she had missed him. "I'm fine, I already said that," she repeated.

Angel studied her for a moment, until Julie had to look away. "Good," he said. "You looked so tired that I wondered."

"You do a lot of work at the center," she said, trying to lighten the mood. "Your absence left a very big hole. You should see the circles under Connie's eyes."

Angel returned her smile and then drained his mug. Julie felt a twinge of disappointment when he rose, but realized that he must be exhausted, with the three-hour time difference.

"I'll see you in the morning," he said, turning at the door. "Unless you want to sleep awhile and come in later?"

She shook her head, already looking forward to being there and knowing that he, too, was somewhere close by. "That's not necessary. Besides, you might have some questions."

"Okay."

He moved closer, and she thought he was going to kiss her, but he only trailed a fiery path down her cheek with his fingers. He tipped up her chin and smiled down into her face while Julie did her best not to read too much into his warm expression. After he told her goodnight, she stood on the porch until the taillights of his Ferrari disappeared around the corner. Then she wandered back inside. For the first night in a week, she slept soundly and woke refreshed the next morning.

While she was munching on whole-grain toast and coffee, Angel sat at his kitchen table eating the egg-and-cheese omelette that Joey put before him. "Did you hear Luis come in last night?" he asked as Joey poured coffee and sat down across from Angel with his own breakfast.

"No, but it must have been late. I think he's sleeping now."

Angel sipped his juice. "Yeah. It's no secret that he doesn't get up till noon. But I thought he might make an effort my first day back."

Joey didn't comment, spooning salsa onto his eggs.

"Maybe he'll come to the center later," Angel said.

"Maybe so."

For long moments they ate in silence, then Joey rose to take the dirty plates. "More coffee?" he asked.

"No, thanks. Joey, are you happy here?"

The other man looked surprised, then wary. "Yeah, I guess. Why, do you want me to leave?"

Angel almost laughed. "No, man. I just wondered how you're doing."

Joey leaned one sturdy hip against the counter, looking distinctly uncomfortable. "Do you like Connie?" he asked, staring down at his fingernails.

Angel hid his surprise. "Do I like her how? As a secretary? A friend? A woman?"

Joey's earnest gaze met Angel's. "Do you think she'd ever go for someone like me?" he asked.

At last Angel understood. Joey's ego had taken a powerful blow when Maria left him, and then another when he had lost his job at the machining plant. Angel stood and walked around the table, clapping his friend on the shoulder. "I think she'd be damned lucky if a *hombre* like you took an interest in her," he said.

Joey shrugged. "Yeah, thanks. Right now I just don't have much to offer anyone."

Angel knew what he meant. "Why don't you come down and talk to our job placement volunteer?" he said. "I know you couldn't find anything as great as working for me, but you could check out what's available."

Joey grinned hugely. "You wouldn't be upset?"

"No, man. I wouldn't be upset."

When Angel left for the center a few minutes later, Luis still hadn't put in an appearance, but Joey was whistling as he cleaned up the kitchen.

Later in the day, as Angel was returning from lunch, he heard an angry stream of Spanish coming from Connie's office.

"I tried to tell you nicely, but you wouldn't take the hint," she continued in English. "I'm not interested in you that way. I like someone else."

Angel's heart sank with disappointment for Joey as he paused in the hallway, wondering how to make his presence known.

"Don't be so uppity, *Concetta*. Your husband's been cold in the ground for a long time now, and what you need in your bed is a real man."

The familiar voice wasn't the one that Angel had expected to hear, and he leaned against the wall, sick with shock as he realized who had spoken the insulting words.

Chapter Ten

I don't need you!" Connie's words came clearly through the partially closed door. "Stay away from me, Luis."

"Or what?" he taunted. "You'll squeal to my little brother? It won't do you any good. Princess Julie already tried it, and he didn't believe her."

Angel's body went rigid as he listened, sick with rage and shame, to his brother's words. Obviously the time to make excuses for Luis was long past; it was time to face the truth. And how had Luis found out about Julie? He must have been listening.

Fighting down his disbelief and aching disillusionment, Angel took several deep breaths, trying to deal with what he had just learned. He didn't dare confront Luis before regaining control of his temper, or he was sure to do something that would make the situation even worse. Angel doubted that was possible, but moments before he wouldn't have believed Luis could be such a creep, either.

Only the repeated reminders to himself that Luis was all the family he had, kept Angel in the hallway until Connie's voice, higher and tinged with fear, forced him to act.

"Leave me alone!" she said sharply.

Angel knocked on the door, pushing it open. He forced himself to smile blandly at the other two as their heads swiveled on hearing his entrance. Tension in the room was thick as a Seattle fog as Luis straightened away from Connie, who was standing behind her chair.

"Hi, Luis," Angel said, ignoring the other man's scowl. "Nice of you to make it down. I must have missed you this morning." He made himself shake Luis's hand, although he would have rather punched him.

Then he looked at Connie, whose cheeks were flaming with agitation. "Did you get to the bank yet?" he asked, staring at her in silent communication.

For a moment she looked blank. "The bank?" Then comprehension dawned. "Oh, the bank. I forgot. Mind if I take a late lunch on the way?" Her speech was rushed, and she was clearly more rattled by the incident with Luis than she wanted to let on. "I need to pick up a birthday present for Ernesto. He'll be three on Saturday."

A muscle twitched in Angel's cheek. "Sure, Connie. Take all the time you need."

After he watched her grab her purse, cutting a wide circle around Luis as she crossed to the door, Angel turned his attention to his brother as if he were looking at a stranger. What had happened to the big hero who had bought Angel ice cream and protected him from bullies? It was beginning to appear that he had turned into a bully himself. Then Angel remembered the times that Luis hadn't acted much like a hero, the times he had ignored his little brother or worse. Perhaps Angel himself had been trying too hard to turn Luis into a plaster saint, forgetting the other side to his complex personality. Angel fully intended to give Luis a fair hearing, but before he could speak, the phone rang.

"Come on into my office while I get that," Angel said.

Picking up the receiver, he listened grimly to the panic-stricken voice on the line. It was one of the younger men who had been coming in for literacy instruction and job placement aid. He was at the hospital emergency room with a broken arm.

"I have to go," he told Luis after he assured Robert that he would be there soon.

Luis was slouched against the doorjamb, hands in his pockets. Only his eyes gave him away. For the first time Angel noticed that they glittered with resentment.

Angel explained the problem quickly. "Want to ride along?"

Luis shook his head. "I'll wait around here."

Angel hated to go, wanting to tell him to leave Connie alone, and Julie, too, when she returned. Frustrated, he said instead, "There's trash upstairs that needs to be hauled to the dump if you have the time."

Luis made no response.

"This might take a while. If you get tired of waiting, perhaps we can get caught up over dinner tonight."

"I dunno," Luis said. "I sorta made plans."

Angel forced down a rapid surge of temper. "Can you sorta postpone them? I'll be home by six at the latest."

Luis's shrug bordered on insolence. "I suppose so."

Angel had to be content with that. After scribbling a note to Connie and switching on the answering machine, he drove to the hospital, rubbing one hand across his forehead, which was beginning to ache.

There was no time to dwell on Luis now; he had Robert to deal with. Then he had to figure out how to make amends to Julie for not believing her. Rapping out an angry oath, he slammed one fist against the steering wheel as he turned into the hospital parking lot. Welcome home, Angel, he muttered through clenched teeth.

Julie got back to the office from a meeting with the local junior high school principal much later than she had expected. Dumping a pile of folders and pamphlets onto her desk, she called out a greeting to Connie and asked if Angel was around.

"He left a note," Connie replied. "He may not be back today at all." She explained where he had gone.

"That's okay," Julie said, pausing in the doorway. "I don't have the stats he wanted for his meeting with Bourne Logging. I think I'll finish up at home and give them to him in the morning."

"He's not coming in before the meeting," Connie said. "He's going directly there."

"Did he mention my report before he left?" It wasn't like Angel to forget about something that important. Bourne was thinking about hiring several unskilled laborers from the center, as well as making a monetary donation.

Connie looked agitated. She must have had a hectic day herself. "No," she said. "I wasn't here when he left, and the answering machine was already on."

Julie did a fast calculation in her head. "There's no other way," she said. "It'll take me a while to finish this. I'll just run it out to Angel's house when I'm done so he has it for the morning.''

If Connie thought her plan odd, she gave no indication. She seemed to be preoccupied, but Julie knew she had been planning a big, family birthday party for that weekend. Perhaps she was thinking about the arrangements.

''You have his address?'' Connie asked.

Julie nodded self-consciously. ''He lives close to my parents. I know the house.''

''Good.'' The phone rang and Connie reached to answer it. Relieved, Julie went back to her hot and stuffy office to gather the materials she needed. She had missed lunch, and her stomach was beginning to make hungry noises. All she wanted was a salad and a tall glass of iced tea, then some time with no distractions to get the work done. She had mixed feelings about showing up at Angel's unannounced, even with a valid reason, but it couldn't be helped. He had invited her to take a tour, and maybe the offer was still open.

While Julie was finishing her salad, Stef stopped by. She and Tom had decided that they were meant to be friends but nothing more. Even though it had been mutual, Stef needed a sympathetic ear, and someone to tell her she had done the right thing.

''We enjoy eating lunch together and talking about work, but we've both realized that there's no romantic spark between us,'' she explained, sipping from a tall, sweating glass of iced tea and lemon.

''I'm sorry,'' Julie said, thinking of the paperwork that awaited her, but also of all the times that Stef had listened patiently to her own woes. ''You seemed to get along so well.''

Stef shrugged. "We do. We get along very well, but things just weren't progressing, if you know what I mean. So don't be sorry. Actually, I'm kind of relieved." Her smile looked anything but forced.

"You don't seem heartbroken," Julie commented.

"I was beginning to think something was wrong with me," Stef continued. "But it will be better this way. There's a new guy in accounting—" Her cheeks colored and she glanced down at her tea. "Well, he asked me out, and now I don't have to feel disloyal."

Julie studied her friend's happy expression. Tom had given Stef some much-needed self-confidence, and her initial interest in him had prodded her to take more care with her appearance. Plus she had gained a friend in him, which was a bonus.

"What about you?" Stef said before Julie could ask any questions. "What's happening with you and the boss man?"

Julie glanced at her new wall clock. "As a matter of fact, I had better get to work on a report he needs first thing in the morning, or our relationship might take a definite turn for the worse," she said lightly.

Stef finished her tea and stood up. "You're bringing work home now?"

"This is kind of an unusual situation," Julie said, "but I didn't mean for you to rush off."

"Don't worry. You're busy. I'll just have to pump you some other time." Stef's smile was mischievous. "Don't think you'll evade my questions for long, Julie. I'll call you after my date with John, and we'll have a long talk, okay?"

With a wry smile at her friend's persistence, Julie agreed, following Stef to the door. "We'll get together soon, I promise."

The report took longer than she had thought it would, and she debated calling before she drove out to Angel's house, then decided against it. If he was out or busy, she could leave the papers with Joey. That would probably be better, anyway.

Her feelings toward Angel were stronger than ever, but she didn't know what to do about them, and she sensed that his emotions, if he felt any, were kept firmly in check. Until she had some idea how he really felt about her, it might be wiser to keep her distance.

That seemed like a sensible idea until she drove out to his house. After sitting parked in the circular driveway for several minutes, gathering her courage, she grabbed the report and marched up to the imposing double front doors. When she rang the bell, Angel came to answer it himself. The light from the entryway backlit his powerful frame. He was dressed, as he so often was, in tight, worn jeans and a blue chambray shirt with the collar turned up. With his face in a shadow, Julie couldn't read his expression until he turned on the porch light.

He looked tired, and his hair was mussed as if he'd been raking his fingers through it.

"What are you doing here?" he asked, smiling slowly as if he had awakened from a bad dream. He stretched out a hand, urging her closer. Automatically she took a step back, holding the file folder out to him.

"It's the figures you wanted for the meeting in the morning," she said. "I just finished them."

He took it from her. "You didn't have to bring it out here."

"Connie said you weren't coming in before the meeting."

He rubbed a hand across his forehead. "You're right. I probably would have gotten clear up past Sedro

Woolley before I gave it a thought. Come in." He stepped back, holding the door wide.

"Weren't you busy?" she stalled, wanting to go inside but not sure it would be wise.

"No." There was an edge to his voice she didn't understand. "I was waiting for Luis, but he's still out somewhere."

She had assumed that the Chevy Luis usually drove was in the triple car garage that joined the house at an angle, even though Angel's Ferrari was parked outside. "It's late."

"Please," he coaxed, "you've never seen the house, and the least I can do is offer you coffee, or a drink."

She finally stepped past him, looking around curiously. "How's Robert's arm?"

"It's in a cast, but I helped him with the paperwork and followed him home. He'll be okay."

He slipped off her lightweight jacket and hung it in a closet in the big hall. "Come on," he said, threading his fingers through hers. "I'll give you the tour and then some coffee."

"Where's Joey?" She could hear music coming from the back of the large house.

"Joey left for Connie's right after dinner. She had kind of a rough day." Julie waited, but Angel didn't elaborate. "And Luis said something earlier about having plans."

Julie noticed a certain grimness when he mentioned his brother. Before she had time to ask about it, Angel had paused in the arched doorway of what was obviously the living room.

"This is beautiful," she exclaimed, looking at the leather furniture, Navaho rugs and southwestern paintings. The whole room was done in soft desert tones, with brighter accents in the rugs and pillows. A tall cactus in a terra-cotta pot stood guard in one corner, and instead of drapes, lightweight shades covered the windows. A fireplace on the far wall was finished in adobe bricks with a hearth of glazed tiles.

Angel saw her looking at it. "I had the fireplace redone," he said. "It was too formal before."

"The whole room looks so inviting, and yet there's an elegance about it, too," she said.

Angel tugged at her hand. "Come on, I'll show you the rest."

Julie fell in love with the kitchen, which was vast enough for a party, but so well organized that two people could work together on an intimate supper.

Along the hall, its floor covered in unglazed tiles, Angel pointed out a powder room and more closets. Then he led her down two steps to the recreation room that stretched across the back of the house. "This is where I spend my time," he said.

On one wall, behind a wet bar, racing trophies were displayed. On another there was an elaborate stereo system from which a plaintive ballad drifted. A pool table took up part of the room, and a grouping of casual furniture and a large-screen television were at the other end. A huge window, stained-glass panels at either end, framed the night's blackness beyond.

"It's all very lovely," Julie said, her feet sinking into the cocoa-brown carpet. Inadvertently she glanced toward the ceiling.

"Four bedrooms upstairs," Angel said, following the direction of her gaze. "Plus two more baths and a laundry room."

His eyes darkened and his expression became more intimate as he stepped closer, his arm sliding around her waist. "The master bedroom is huge," he murmured, studying her face through narrowed eyes. "And the bath is a decadent fantasy." His free hand reached out to twine in her hair. "You wouldn't believe how sexy black marble can look in the right light."

Julie felt herself going under without even a token struggle, overcome by his nearness. She took a steadying breath and moved out of his loose embrace. "I'll take your word for it," she said brightly, more nervous of her own reaction than of him.

Angel followed her retreat, stalking her like a big cat. "You aren't afraid of me?" he asked, his voice a gentle growl.

Julie shook her head. "No." Her answer lacked conviction, and one hand went to her throat.

"Dare I be so bold as to think you might have missed me?" he asked, taking another step closer. His hand slid around her neck beneath her hair, fingers burrowing into her scalp.

Julie tried hard to concentrate on his question. What was it he had asked? Something about missing him?

His thumb at the point of her jaw pressed gently, urging her chin up. Julie frowned slightly, trying to formulate a coherent reply.

Had she missed him? "Yes," she breathed, unaware she had spoken aloud until she saw the flash of satisfaction deep in his blue eyes.

He was close, so close. Somewhere in the room there was a tiny click as the music tape ran out. The silence in the big house was emphasized by their breathing—his shallow, waiting; hers rapid, as she stared in fascination at his mouth. Her hands lifted to his chest, warm and hard beneath the soft fabric of his shirt.

For a moment his eyes closed as if in pain. She pulled back, and his lids flared open, his intent stare imprisoning her like a butterfly on a pin. His fingers tightened against her scalp as his head lowered. Their only other point of contact was the joining of their mouths. Powerless, Julie returned his insistent kiss, her hands hovering and then returning to his chest before they slid down around his narrow waist.

On the edge of her awareness she felt him grasp her hip as he eased a hard thigh between her legs, surging against her with an intimacy that exploded through her quivering body. Then she lost track of everything except the heat of his mouth and the seductive movement of his hips.

For a moment Angel tried to hold on to sanity, remembering that there was something he must say to her. Luis, something about Luis. Ah, yes. An apology. Julie had come to him for help and he had failed her. He tore his mouth from hers, intending to explain, to make amends.

Julie made a small whimpering sound in her throat. Then, eyes shut, she sought his mouth for another kiss. As she strained toward him, soft lips touching his, Angel abandoned his noble intentions and gave in to his passion.

There would be time for talk later. Holding her tight against him, he shuddered with the wild need that tore at his control. Her hands dug into his back as she buried her face against his shoulder. Murmuring encouragement, he scooped her into his arms and turned in the direction of the curving staircase.

"Cara mia," he breathed against her ear. "Stay with me. I need you so."

He took the kisses she strung along his jaw as agreement. Once inside the vast master suite, he triumphantly kicked the door shut behind them and set her on her feet, letting her slide down his aroused body as slowly as melting ice cream. A single light burned beside the wide bed in the room he had subconsciously decorated with her in mind.

Julie had an impression of warmth and space and soft welcoming colors before Angel pulled her back into his embrace. "Will you stay?" he asked again, the glow of his narrowed eyes screened by his thick black lashes. His face was taut, as if he was under a great strain, and his arms circled her tightly, almost hurting her with their strength.

Julie nodded shyly, unable to deny his need or her own. There was much between them to be worked out, but this was not the time for that. This was a time for love, for fulfilling desires and making dreams come true.

Angel began to unbutton her blouse, his touch warm against her flesh. Her fingers went to the snaps down the front of his shirt. After she released them, she pulled it free of his jeans and slid her palms across his hot, bare skin.

"I want you so much," he said softly. "I was longing for you, and you came to me."

I love you, she whispered in her heart. Out loud she said, "I'm glad. I want you, too."

He stripped away her cotton shirt. "Show me, sweet Julianna. Show me how much you want me." His voice had thickened, and his hands trembled as he pressed his open mouth to her bare shoulder. Julie's bones melted, and she leaned against him as his hand reached behind him to push the lock on the door. Then he picked her up again and carried her to the bed, following her down onto its softness. His shirt hung open around them, and Julie arched as his hand slid behind her to release her bra.

She helped him remove their clothes, urged on by fierce needs and burning hungers. Both finally free of all barriers, they came together with a power that took Julie's breath away.

As the air hissed between her lips, Angel abruptly went still.

"Did I hurt you? Did I frighten you?"

"Only if you stop," she moaned, hands urging him on, body trembling around him. "Please, Angel. I—need you now." In her agitation she had almost told him how much she loved him. Before she could dwell on the near slip, he surged, scattering her thoughts like dry leaves in a hot desert wind.

His movements were rough, hungry, ragged with determination, and she clung tightly, rising to meet him, giving him everything she had, as he finally did with her, pouring his strength, his very life into her as he chanted her name like a litany.

Julie's heated body was still rippling with aftershocks as he collapsed against her.

"God," he muttered after a few moments, flopping onto his back and wrapping an arm around her to pull her close, "you strip me bare and drain me. You take everything, and give more." His free hand lifted to brush the hair off her forehead. "If I ever recover, we have to talk."

Julie snuggled against his broad chest, reluctant to break the spell of enchantment that surrounded them. Her fingers wandered over his moist, heated skin as she savored his words. She didn't want to talk or to think, she wanted only to feel his power and his tenderness.

After a minute his fingers captured hers, and he raised them to his mouth. One by one he took them inside, tugging gently. Julie felt the erotic caress to the depths of her being. She shifted restlessly, desire rising again like a flood tide.

Angel raised up on one elbow. "Greedy, little one?" he asked with tender amusement.

Blushing, Julie glanced away, unable to voice her new hungers.

Angel took her hand and skimmed it down his body. Her fingers circled him gently as he groaned.

"I'm greedy," he whispered. "I want a night of love with you."

Love, Julie thought. Of that she had so much to give him. She turned in his arms and he bent to her, mouth covering hers.

Afterward they slept. Several more times in the night they awakened and reached for each other with eager hands and ardent mouths. Finally Julie awoke again and the room was lighter. Beside her, Angel slept like the dead, or the completely satiated. She stroked his midnight-dark hair with fingers that trembled, before she eased her pleasantly aching body from the bed.

He awoke to the sound of running water. Stretching, he contemplated joining her in the shower, but all that they needed to discuss rose in his mind like a dam.

Angel was at the window looking out over the garden when he heard Julie pad softly into the room. He turned almost reluctantly, knowing what he had to say, but not sure how to begin.

The sight of her wrapped in one of his oversized bath sheets distracted him from his thoughts and he quickly crossed the room to take her in his arms.

"Good morning," he said, kissing her lips. To his surprise, she struggled from his embrace, her gaze searching his face. Then, as he returned her silent stare, a light seemed to die in her hazel eyes.

"Good morning," she echoed, dropping her gaze.

Angel continued to stare, willing her to give him a sign that the night before had meant as much to her as it had to him. Instead, she glanced worriedly toward the front of the house. "I had no intentions of staying the night. Your neighbors will be getting up soon."

Angel tried to swallow his disappointment. Was she so ashamed of what they had shared that she was afraid someone would see her leaving? Even though he wasn't all that eager to talk about his manipulative brother, Angel knew that he needed to clear the air with her.

Hell, he didn't even want to think about Luis right now. Angel still hadn't figured out how to explain his own bad judgement to Julie in a way that she would understand and forgive. His feelings toward her were in turmoil. Finding himself where he had sworn he would never be again—emotionally involved with her—he wondered if it would be best if he took some time to think things through.

Julie watched the changes on his expressive face as she waited for the words that didn't come. Words she needed so desperately to hear. She had been foolish to think that another night in bed with Angel would draw a declaration of love from him that he obviously didn't feel. On top of everything, if she didn't get out of there quickly, she would be running into Joey or a smirking Luis on the stairs. With Angel's love, she could face anyone, but without it she felt like a rumpled one-night stand.

Hurriedly she grabbed her clothes and began to dress, back turned to Angel. She heard the sound of denim sliding up his body, and when she turned he was shrugging into a shirt. His expression was not that of a man about to pour out his heart.

"I have to go," she said when he still didn't speak. No point in hanging around waiting for words that weren't coming.

"Can I at least offer you coffee?" he asked, "or don't you have the time even for that?"

How could she stay, wanting to hear so badly what he wasn't going to say? "No, thank you," she refused politely. "I really have to go."

Angel saw her to the door in his bare feet, picking up the morning paper as she hesitated on the porch.

"I'll see you at the office," she told him, allowing herself one last searching glance into his closed, brooding face.

"Yeah, after the meeting." He was obviously already preoccupied with other thoughts. Coloring, she glanced around self-consciously, but none of the neighbors appeared to be looking.

As she turned to go, his hand shot out, catching her arm. "Julie," he said as she paused, looking up at him expectantly. "Can't you come back in, have something to eat?"

She did her best to hide her disappointment, shaking her head. The night before seemed like a dream, distant, fading. The closeness they had shared was beginning to blur in the light of day. Tears misted her vision as she got into her car and started the motor, refusing to look back as she went down the driveway.

Behind her, Angel had walked to the edge of the porch and was scowling darkly at the Ferrari, which was parked a good ten feet farther back than he had left it. He didn't really mind Luis borrowing his car; he just hated the stealthy manner in which his brother went about it.

As he walked back into the house to make coffee and read the newspaper, Angel remembered several times when the car had had less gas than he had thought it should. Filling the coffeepot automatically, he wondered how long Luis had been taking the Ferrari, and for what purpose. Perhaps it was time to find out.

A sour smell pinched his nostrils when he opened the door to his brother's room. Angel had showered and dressed in a gray suit for his business meeting. He kicked a booted foot at the clothing that lay everywhere across Luis's floor. Empty beer cans and full ashtrays littered the dresser, and Luis lay in the middle of the unmade bed, fully clothed and snoring.

"Luis! Wake up." Angel tried unsuccessfully to keep the disgust from his voice. He'd been blind for too long, but now he was fed up. He wanted answers.

He walked to the side of the bed and shook Luis's inert body. The snoring grew louder.

"Luis!" Angel shook him harder and finally got a response.

Luis's dark eyes were bloodshot in the dim light as he stared up at Angel. "What the hell?" he croaked.

"We have to talk."

Luis peered at the numbers on his clock radio and groaned. "Later, bro," he said, rolling over.

Angel clamped a hand on his shoulder. "You've got five minutes. Go take a cold shower, and I'll meet you downstairs."

Something in his voice must have penetrated. When he reached to shut the door behind him, Luis had struggled to a sitting position, holding his head in his hands and groaning.

While Angel waited, he sipped at another cup of coffee and glanced through the newspaper. A headline on the front page of the local section caught his attention.

Burglars Invade Wealthy Country Club Area.

He read the article, frowning deeply, coffee forgotten. A series of burglaries in his exclusive neighborhood was angering home owners and frustrating police. Before Angel could study the article further, the doorbell rang. The house was silent. Joey must still be sleeping. Slapping the paper down, Angel went to answer the summons himself, wondering who would be coming by that early.

The last thing he expected to see when he yanked open the door was two uniformed deputy sheriffs on the steps.

"Good morning," one said politely, tipping his hat as the other stood back a few paces, hand on the butt of his gun. "Is that your black Ferrari parked there?"

Angel nodded, his guts twisting into a painful knot.

"We'd like to ask you a few questions."

Angel glanced from one serious face to the other. "This isn't a good time," he said, thinking of the talk he needed to have with Luis, and of his meeting later that morning. "Can't it wait?"

"No, sir, it can't. We can talk here or at the station, the choice is up to you."

Behind him, Angel could hear Luis thumping down the staircase. All of Angel's brotherly instincts rose to

the fore, and he pulled the front door shut behind him
"Let's go," he said, to the officers' obvious surprise.

When he turned to look up at the house from the
back of the patrol car, he saw Joey at an upstairs window, face crumpled with worry as he watched Angel
being taken away.

Chapter Eleven

After going home to change clothes and eat breakfast, Julie felt rushed and utterly drained when she arrived at the center. As soon as she had poured herself a mug of coffee from the pot in the kitchen and gotten settled in her office, Connie poked her head through the adjoining door.

"Have you talked to Angel this morning?"

Guilt sharpened Julie's reply. "Why would I talk to Angel? I just got here." She dropped her purse into a desk drawer and pushed it shut. "Besides, he has a meeting. You were the one who told me he wouldn't be in."

Connie's expression was clouded with worry as she came farther into the room. "I know. The manager from Bourne Logging is on the phone. Angel's a half hour late, and he hasn't called them."

"That's not like him," Julie said, wondering what could have happened. "Did you try his house?"

"Not yet, but I will." Connie turned to leave.

"Wait," Julie said impulsively. "Let me call instead."

Connie gave her an odd look. "Okay. I'll delay Mr. Hobbs. Let me know if you find out anything."

"I will," Julie answered absently as she dialed Angel's home number. She was relieved when Joey answered the phone and not Luis.

"I don't know where Angel went," Joey said in reply to her inquiry, but he sounded so nervous that Julie didn't believe him.

"Joey," she said sharply, "what's going on? Angel is late for an important meeting that I can't believe he'd miss if he didn't have to. If you know something, please tell me."

"I don't know if Angel would want me to say anything." Joey's voice was strung tight.

Julie gripped the receiver firmly, shoving down her rising impatience. "Joey," she pleaded, "this is very important."

The silence at the other end was almost enough to make her scream. What was going on? Feeling nervous herself, she tried a different approach. "I know how much you care about Angel. Is he in some kind of trouble? Is he hurt?"

"I don't think I should tell you," Joey repeated stubbornly.

Julie leaped up, pulling the phone cord as she began to pace, anxiety tearing at her. The strong instinct that Angel needed her was enough to make her fling caution aside. "Joey," she said again, more determined than ever, "I know how much you love Angel, how much you've always loved him. I know he would appreciate your loyalty." She swallowed, then forced herself to continue. "But I love him, too, and you're beginning to frighten me. Please tell me what's going on. Perhaps I can help."

"You love him?" Joey echoed.

Julie rolled her eyes and fought for patience. "Yes, I do, believe me. And I promise that I'll come over there and personally strangle you if you don't tell me what's going on!" Her patience had abruptly run out.

"Oh, Julie, I don't know what to do!" Joey's voice rose in panic as he blurted out the last thing Julie had expected to hear. "Angel's been arrested. The police came and took him away in a squad car, and I didn't know who to call, what to do—"

"Arrested? Why?"

"I don't know. Should I go to the station? Should I call the lawyer?" Joey asked. "I didn't know if I should tell anyone."

Julie tried desperately to think clearly. "No, you stay put in case Angel calls there." If he needed bail or a lawyer, she would certainly be of more assistance to him than Joey would, as frightened as he was. "I'm sure this is all just some terrible mistake, but I'll go to the station and see what I can do."

"Gracias," Joey said, the relief in his voice obvious. "First Angel left, then Luis. I was so worried."

"Luis? Didn't he know they'd taken Angel in?" Julie couldn't believe that even a rat like Luis would desert his own flesh and blood.

"Si. I told him myself. When he rushed outside, I asked if he was going after them, but he said he had something important to take care of, and drove off in his car."

"Don't worry," Julie said. "I'll leave right now, and I'll call you as soon as I know something." She hung up the receiver on another string of thank-yous, told Connie she had to go out and not to do anything about Angel until Julie contacted her, then raced downtown.

She had never been inside the police station before, but this was not the time to hover timidly in the doorway. Grasping her bravado with both hands, she approached the first uniformed officer she saw, and he directed her to Detective Jenkins, whose desk was in the middle of a large, unbelievably hectic office.

"How may I help you?" he asked, looking her over with a slightly cynical smile as he showed her to a chair. The detective was a big man in a rumpled suit, with thinning brown hair, a cigarette dangling from his mouth and a world-weary air about him.

"Angel Maneros," she said. "He was arrested this morning, and I have to know why."

"Are you a relative?" His close scrutiny made Julie want to shift nervously and pull her narrow skirt farther over her knees, but she did neither.

"I'm Julianna Remington. We're engaged," she improvised, tucking her bare left hand out of sight.

"I see." Jenkins frowned, then shrugged. "I guess it won't hurt to tell you. Mr. Maneros wasn't arrested. We just wanted to ask him some questions about an ongoing burglary investigation."

"Burglary!" Julie exclaimed. "Was his house broken into?" Funny that Angel hadn't mentioned it to her.

Detective Jenkins shook his head. "You've got it backward. His car was spotted by a witness to a burglary late last night. Unfortunately Mr. Maneros wasn't able to give us an alibi—"

Julie cut him off excitedly without stopping to think of the possible consequences. "He was with me. I mean, I was with him."

"All night?" The detective's expression had turned speculative.

She bobbed her head nervously. He had to believe her. "Yes, we were together all night." Several people turned to stare, and she realized that her voice had risen.

"You have to let him out," she pleaded, grabbing the detective's arm as she saw one uniformed officer elbow another and grin in her direction. "Angel wouldn't steal. He's got money. It must have been another black Ferrari."

"Well, the witness did get a partial license number."

"I spent the whole night with Angel at his house," Julie repeated as another officer approached the desk with some papers. He, too, looked at her with interest as Detective Jenkins took the papers and laid them on top of his cluttered desk. Julie's cheeks flamed, but she didn't care if the whole station knew.

"He didn't slip away, either," she added. "I would have known. I, uh, wasn't asleep."

Detective Jenkins's eyebrows rose. "I see."

She stood, clutching her purse. "Where are you holding him? I can arrange for bail, for a lawyer, whatever he needs. Where is he?"

She didn't like the amusement that flickered in Jenkins's slightly bloodshot eyes as he gazed up at her.

"Hold your horses, Miss Remington. I don't know where he is."

Her mouth dropped open with shock. "You *lost* him?" She couldn't believe their incompetence.

"Not exactly. We let him go."

His words penetrated slowly, and she sank back down into the chair. "What do you mean?"

The detective gave her a long look, as if deciding how much to tell her, while Julie fidgeted under his gaze.

"While we were questioning Mr. Maneros, who came down here by his own choice by the way, we got a call from a local pawnbroker. He had a list of stolen items that we'd circulated from some earlier burglaries, and he had someone in his shop trying to fence some of the goods. Our men picked up the suspect, and we're booking him right now." He clamped his lips shut as if regretting how much he had said.

Julie's chest heaved with relief.

Just then a movement caught the corner of her eye and she turned to see Luis, in handcuffs, come out of another room between two uniformed officers. She stared at him in shock until he turned and their eyes met.

Luis gave her a cocky grin and said something to one of the men escorting him. The officer looked around at Julie who turned abruptly away, back to Detective Jenkins.

"Is that the man you arrested for the burglaries?" she asked in a hoarse whisper.

He followed the direction of her pointing finger.

"Uh, yes. Do you know him?"

She wondered if she would be somehow implicating herself if she admitted that she did. "He's Angel's half brother," she said finally.

"We know that now. When the uniforms radioed in, I excused Mr. Angel Maneros and he left."

Something wasn't right. Angel had gone and left Luis to his fate? "Wait a minute," Julie said. "Was Angel aware of why he was let go?"

The detective shrugged, obviously reluctant to say more. "I don't know."

"Wasn't he told that his brother had been arrested?" She couldn't imagine Angel abandoning Luis, no matter how hurt and upset he might be.

Detective Jenkins scratched his bony chin. "No, come to think about it, I don't imagine that he did know. He was gone before they brought the brother in."

Julie leaped to her feet. "I have to find him. What's going to happen to Luis?"

"He won't be going anywhere, don't you worry." The detective smiled. Julie was beginning to wonder about the man's sense of humor.

"Oh. I understand." She had to find Angel and tell him before he heard somewhere else. "Thank you for your help," she said belatedly.

"Yes, ma'am, and best wishes with the wedding."

For a moment Julie went blank. Wedding? Then she remembered and managed a shaky smile. "Thank you again." Tucking her left hand into her pocket, she rushed out, stopping at a pay phone to call Joey. After she explained what had happened, and learned that he still hadn't heard from Angel, she asked him to call Connie and bring her up to date. Then Julie went looking for Angel.

She drove around for a half hour, checking all the places he might have gone. She called both Joey and Connie again to see if they had heard from him, went past her own apartment and was about to give up when she remembered one place she hadn't tried.

"Of course," she said aloud, making an illegal U-turn. "Why didn't I think of it before?"

Angel was sitting on a log, watching the river drift by and wondering what to do next. His suit jacket lay next to him, and he'd pulled the knot of his tie loose. The first two buttons of his shirt were open, and a trickle of perspiration ran down the side of his neck.

He had driven by the house as soon as the police broke off their questioning, but Luis's Chevy was already gone, and Angel hadn't taken the time to stop. He'd been all over town, soon realizing that he wasn't aware enough of his brother's habits to really know where to look. Luis could be anywhere.

Angel scuffed at a clump of weeds with the toe of his boot and wished he had a cigarette. The spot on the riverbank where he and Julie used to come when they were in high school was so overgrown that he could barely see the water from the dirt road where he had left the car. Other than that, the area was almost the same as it had been way back then.

Angel's mood was black. Julie didn't really care about him; that was clear by the hasty way she had left him that morning. Good Lord, had it only been hours before? It seemed like days had gone by since he'd held her in his arms and tried to convey all he felt toward her.

She might not love him, but she probably liked the way he made her feel in bed, and perhaps it was gratifying to her, too, that she could still put him through hoops after so much time had passed. She certainly knew how to wring every drop of life out of him, making him feel like he'd died and gone to heaven when she opened her arms and her body to him. He got hard just thinking about her, despite his worry and anger toward Luis.

Face it, you dumb half-breed, he told himself. You're still someone she can't, or won't, make a commitment to. Even if her ex-husband abused her, he still had the right blood in his veins and the right background. Compared to that, what do you have but a notorious past and an uncertain future?

He tossed aside the long spear of grass he'd been chewing. After all they had been through, she still held back all that was really important.

Idly, he pulled several more long stalks of grass loose from a clump next to his foot and inserted the tip of one between his lips as the sun beat down on him and the breeze ruffled his hair. He remembered the way Julie had been in high school, so utterly trusting. At first he had been skeptical that anyone could love and accept him the way she had. She hadn't seen the poverty, the mixed blood, the illegitimate background. She had looked into his eyes and seen his soul. And she had loved him. Utterly and unconditionally, as he had loved her.

Then he had finally asked too much of her, and lost her. He sighed deeply, remembering that Luis was the one he should be thinking about now. It was beginning to look like Luis might need Angel more than ever.

Angel had been trying to convince himself that Luis couldn't have anything to do with the burglaries. It was true that he had gone on about getting a stake and leaving town, but Angel had believed it was only the beer talking. Now he wasn't sure what to think.

Luis had secretly taken his car, but then Luis had never tried to hide his preference for Angel's Ferrari over his own used Chevy. Even the article in the paper and the witness's partial identification of a license plate number could have just been part of a series of unfortunate coincidences.

So why did things feel so wrong?

When the police had arrived on the doorstep, Angel had clung to his belief in Luis's innocence, but he had still gone down to the station rather than subject Luis to questioning. When he had heard all the facts, he'd tried not to think at all. No matter how serious things looked, he couldn't lose faith in Luis before they had a chance to straighten it all out. If only he could find his brother and talk to him. Angel hadn't said a word to the detective who had questioned him. It would have been disloyal. Luis was still his brother, the only family he had left since his beloved mother had stepped into the path of a murderous drunk and taken the knife cut meant for someone else.

Angel's head sank into his hands as he slumped forward on the log, wondering what he could have done differently.

"I'm sorry, Mama," he murmured, but the words drifted away on the gentle breeze that rippled through the tall grasses along the riverbank. Angel knew she didn't hear him.

He rose and paced the muddy edge of the water, raking one hand through his hair repeatedly. Where could Luis have gone? Would he have left town? No, one thing Angel hadn't given him was a lot of cash. He'd meant to make some arrangements eventually, when Luis settled in better, but the more disillusioned Angel had become, the easier it had been to keep putting it off.

Perhaps if he hadn't been so wrapped up in his growing feelings for Julie...

No, if anything, he had messed that up good by going too far the other way. When Julie had come to him with her worries about Luis, he hadn't even listened. Instead he had brushed aside her complaints, refusing to hear anything bad about his precious brother. Angel thought of the accusations he had hurled at Julie at the time, and felt sick inside.

He bent and picked up a flat rock, remembering when Luis had showed him how to skip them across the water. With an angry oath, Angel flung it far out over the slowly meandering river. Resentment toward Luis and the position he had put Angel in was beginning to rise. Had he used the Ferrari to deliberately throw suspicion Angel's way? Could Luis be that rotten?

Luis would have been smarter to use his own car; it would have commanded less attention. He had wanted Angel to buy him something newer, flashier, but Angel had stalled, ignoring the glow of anger in Luis's eyes when his request was denied. Angel had planned on surprising him with one when he made a real commitment to the center, or found another job, but that hadn't happened.

The thought of the center reminded Angel of his meeting at Bourne Logging. He glanced at his watch with little interest. It was too late now. They must know he wasn't coming.

Later he would have to explain the best he could, apologize. Maybe they would give him another chance. A family emergency, he would say. They would assume he meant an illness, a minor problem of some sort.

How would they react if he told them, "Sorry, I couldn't make it. I was being questioned for some burglaries that my brother probably committed while he was driving my car. You understand how these family problems can pop up at the most inconvenient times."

A snort of derisive laughter echoed in Angel's ears as he stood with his fists jammed into the pockets of his slacks. He realized with a start that it had come from him. Who was he trying to kid with his money and his

success? He was still that little bastard from the wrong
end of town, the one people drew back from as if he
smelled bad.

He whirled, determined to do something, anything,
even if he had to drive up and down every street of
Clarkson, Burlington and Mount Vernon until he found
Luis and got some answers. He had wasted enough time
moping over things it was too late to change.

As he pushed through the tall grass and underbrush
to where he'd parked his car, he heard someone coming through from the road. Probably kids, since he
hadn't even heard another car. Angel parted some alder branches and came face to face with Julie, her hair
in a tangle and her eyes huge with concern.

"Thank God I found you," she said breathlessly,
noting his taut face and the angry line of his mouth.
"I've been looking everywhere."

As she caught her breath and almost swayed with relief, Angel's brows came together in a thunderous
frown. "Why would you possibly be looking for me?"
Then his features formed into the mockery of a smile.
"Ahh, I know, the meeting I missed."

He clearly didn't know yet that Luis had been arrested.

"We have to talk," she said, wondering desperately
where to start. "Is the log still there?" If she didn't sit
down soon, she would collapse.

His frown reappeared but he nodded. She brushed
past him, glancing back impatiently. "Come on," she
urged, pausing until he began to follow her.

"What's all this about? This morning you couldn't
get away fast enough, now you want to chat. I have
other business to take care of," he said arrogantly.

"I went to the station," she said, ignoring his hostile tone.

That got his attention. He stopped in his tracks, one thick brow raised in silent inquiry.

"When the people from the logging company called to say that you hadn't shown up, I talked to Joey."

Angel remained silent.

"It took a lot of convincing on my part before he would tell me what happened. He's very loyal to you." She paused. "At least he told me what he thought had happened," she amended.

"Which was what?" He was so cold and unapproachable that he made her want to shiver in the warm sun.

"Joey thought you had been arrested. Detective Jenkins told me—"

"You talked to Detective Jenkins?" he asked disbelievingly.

"Yes, at the police station."

Angel's expression was changing, the forbidding line of his mouth softening slightly.

"Anyway, Detective Jenkins told me you didn't have an alibi for the robbery last night." She flushed darkly when she remembered how she had almost shouted the station down, telling him just where Angel had been, and whom he had been with. "He let me go on and on about where we were," she said, "before he bothered to tell me that you had already been released."

Angel grabbed her arm. "Wait a minute. You told him that you had been with me?"

"Uh-huh. I told him and practically everyone else down there that I had spent the night with you."

A broad grin spread across his face, and he pulled her into his arms, catching her off guard so that she fell heavily against him before she could brace herself.

"Julie! I thought you were ashamed of our relationship, that you didn't want anyone to know."

It was her turn to be surprised. "Ashamed! Why would you have a crazy idea like that?"

"The way you sneaked out of my house this morning, so afraid the neighbors would see your car."

She would have laughed at his misconception if it wasn't so tragic. "No," she said, pulling out of his embrace, "you have it all wrong. I was embarrassed that I would run into Joey or Luis. I haven't had a lot of experience sneaking out of my lover's bedroom in the morning," she confessed. "I didn't know what I would say if I saw them." While Angel was thinking over her reply, she sat down on the log. After a moment he sat next to her.

"You aren't ashamed of me? Of us?"

His questions sent hope spiraling through her. "Is there an us?" she asked quietly.

Angel leaned closer, facing her, his brilliant eyes glittering with something she dared not put a name to. "There is if you want it that way."

Julie touched her finger to his lips. His expression was unbelievably tender, his hands gentle as they stroked her arms.

"I've never wanted anything else," she whispered, throat thick with emotion. "Even when I thought I was doing the best thing for both of us, my heart was breaking." She waited to see how he would react to her bringing up the past.

He took her hand in his and lifted it to his mouth, kissing her knuckles and then flicking his tongue across the sensitive skin of her palm.

"We have to talk, I mean really talk about that last day," he said, rubbing their linked fingers down his cheek. His eyes darkened as he studied her. "But right now, what I need more than anything is to kiss you."

His voice made Julie's heart ache with tenderness, and when he hesitated, she drew his head down to hers.

Their lips met in a kiss filled with expectation, a gentle sealing of promises to be made and kept. Julie was just beginning to let go of reason and sink into a lovely pool of sensation when she remembered why she had been looking for Angel in the first place. She jerked away so abruptly that he almost went over backward.

"Luis!" she gasped as he righted himself.

Angel's head spun around as if he expected the other man to pop out from behind a bush. "Where?"

She gripped his hands in hers and stared earnestly into his slightly dazed eyes. "That's what I came to tell you about in the first place." She faltered, hating the way his look of quiet happiness turned into something tense and expectant.

"What about Luis?" he urged.

"Oh, Angel, I don't know how to tell you this, but Luis has been arrested."

His reaction surprised her. His shoulders slumped and he shook his head, raking his hair back with one hand. "It's true, then," he muttered, clearly resigned. "I had hoped to find him first."

He stood, fists clenched and head thrown back, fighting the pain. Julie rose beside him, concerned at his reaction to her news.

"Damn," he groaned through clenched teeth. "I prayed it wasn't true." When he looked at her, there was moisture in his blue eyes, and unbearable sorrow.

Julie stroked his arm, feeling helpless against his grief. "Did you already know?" she asked gently.

"I suspected, but I didn't want to believe it. Where did they find him? How did it happen?" He had regained his steely self-control and was looking at her with an unreadable expression, part of him closed off. "I've been searching for him half the morning."

Julie took a deep breath and pushed back the lock of hair that had fallen across his forehead. She really hated telling him the rest, but there was no way she could keep it from him. "Apparently he was trying to sell some of the things from an earlier burglary. The man at the pawnshop called the police, and they picked him up right there."

She felt sick inside, seeing the pinched look around Angel's mouth and the way his nostrils flared with pain. "I saw him at the station," she made herself continue. "That's how I knew you hadn't been told. I was sure that you wouldn't have left him there, and Detective Jenkins confirmed that you didn't know."

"Did you speak to him? How did he seem?"

"I only saw him from a distance. They were booking him, I think." She reached up to stroke his cheek, hating the chill in his eyes. "Angel, he needs you now."

"He's never needed me." His voice was bitter.

"Don't discount all you tried to do, just because he didn't accept your help. He's the fool, not you."

"It didn't help."

"That's not your fault." She wanted to hold him, to share the hurt, but she was sure he would pull away. He seemed to be holding himself in check by the thinnest of threads.

"You don't think I'm a fool?" he asked.

"No, darling. I think you're wonderful to care so much."

His gaze touched hers briefly in silent thanks before his expression hardened again, a muscle twitching in his cheek.

"He does need you now more than ever," she said, "and perhaps he realizes that." She hated to think of Luis taking advantage of Angel again, but knew it couldn't be helped. "Go to the station and see him," she urged. "We can talk later."

He pulled her to him, and she felt a hard shudder ripple through his fiercely taut body before he let her go again. "You'll wait?" he asked.

She thought a moment while he stared down at her, unblinking. "I'll meet you back at my apartment, okay? Straightening things out with Luis may take a while. I'll call Connie and Joey. They're both worried."

He nodded. "Thank you."

She hugged him hard. "I'll be waiting for you."

His arms wrapped around her. "I can't lose you again," he confessed.

She managed a smile. "You won't," she vowed. "Now go to Luis."

He scooped up his suit jacket, then hesitated. "About you and Luis," he began. "I owe you an apology—"

Julie shook her head. "Don't apologize for wanting to think the best of him."

He held out his hand. "You coming?"

Julie looked around at the blue sky and the slowly meandering river. "No. I want to sit here a moment and savor all the memories we have of this place."

His eyes went dark, and his mouth quirked into a smile that was blatantly sexy. "I remember," he said, voice heavy with meaning. "Do you know how difficult it is to leave you now?"

"I know. Take care of Luis, and then we'll take care of us."

"You promise?"

"I promise."

She watched him go, delighting as always at the broad stretch of his shoulders in the tailored dress shirt, the long, smoothly working muscles of his legs sheathed in narrow slacks and the graceful way he moved as he made his way back to their parked cars. When he disappeared from sight, she turned her mind loose to remember the last time they had met on that spot, the last time she had seen him before he went away.

The first time they had made love.

Angel had been talking crazily about running away together ever since his mother's funeral. At first Julie had tried to talk him out of it, and then for a while she had gotten caught up in his enthusiasm, his plans for their future. After the first flush of excitement faded, her cautious nature had reasserted itself and she realized what a small chance she and Angel had—two teenagers without money or a high school diploma between them—out in the big world, far away from family and friends.

It was then she decided to do whatever was necessary to keep Angel in Clarkson. She planned it carefully, insisting that he meet her at their secret place late one sunny afternoon. The very air shimmered with the warmth of an early spring, and the sky was so blue that it didn't look real, almost as blue as Angel's eyes.

When she heard his car pull up, Julie had already spread a blanket across the soft grass of a spot hidden from the road and the river by a stand of alder and tall weeds. Nervously she rubbed her damp palms together, repeating to herself that she was doing the best thing, the only thing possible to bind Angel so tightly to her that when she told him she wasn't going he would have no choice but to stay.

"Julie?" Even his voice sent shivers of awareness through her sensitized body.

"I'm here," she called out softly, bending to turn on the portable radio she had brought.

Angel made his way to the small clearing, careful not to break a path that would alert others to the place's existence. As always when he saw her, his eyes glowed, and his mouth curved into a tender smile.

Julie went into his open arms. Finally, after months of longing, she was going to learn the full measure of his love and become a woman. Everything was happening according to plan.

"I missed you," she said, raising her lips for his kiss.

Angel covered her mouth with his, and she could almost feel his inner struggle to take things slowly and stay in control. Usually Julie cooperated, savoring his kisses while keeping a part of herself separate. Today was different. Today she poured her love into every kiss, each caress of his lean frame, as Angel lowered her to the blanket and followed her down, hands shaking.

"Whoa, baby," he groaned after a few heated moments as her fingers slipped beneath the hem of his T-shirt to stroke the bare skin of his stomach. "I'm not made of steel, you know.'' They both had a good idea of how far they could go before pulling back. Always before, if Julie didn't call a halt, Angel would himself.

She snuggled closer, inching her fingers up to the warmth of his bare chest as her lips nibbled at the corner of his mouth.

Angel's breath sucked in hard as his unsteady hands locked onto her upper arms. When he held her away from him, the battle he was fighting was plain to see on his face. ''You're driving me nuts,'' he said. ''I need a cigarette and a breather or it'll be too late to stop at all.''

Julie gazed up at him pleadingly. Seducing Angel was proving to be easy. His cheeks were flushed, and his eyes burned with desire. ''Let's not stop,'' she whispered, burying her face in his neck and savoring his special scent. ''I love you, Angel.''

He pulled abruptly away, searching her face. ''You mean it? Are you sure you don't want to wait like we planned?''

She had never heard his voice break before. Tenderness washed through her, and she had to subdue a smile. Later he would see the wisdom of her decision and thank her for making him stay. Besides, she couldn't wait any longer, she needed him too desperately.

She nodded slowly, wetting her lips with the tip of her tongue as she trailed her hand across the hard muscles of his thigh. ''I want you,'' she said boldly, watching the way his chest rose and fell.

Tenderly he laid her back against the blanket. ''I'll make it good for you,'' he promised, releasing the buttons of her blouse.

And it was good. She couldn't help but respond to Angel's youthful passion. He swept her along on a tide of physical pleasure that was far beyond anything she had dreamed possible. At one point he turned away, digging into the pocket of his discarded jeans.

"This was for just in case," he said, turning back with a small packet between his fingers. His eyes were earnest. "Just in case we changed our minds, like now."

At one point there was pain, but he was so gentle as he led her through love's intimate dance that it was over in an instant. Then she knew his complete possession.

Sweat stood out on his forehead. "I love you," he chanted as a red mist filled Julie's mind, and her body finally exploded into a series of tremors. "I love you."

She held him tight as the passion that had been building in him for months burst forth, and she was awed by the power of his love.

Afterward they dressed and held each other close, Angel's hand stroking her back. "I'm sorry I had to hurt you," he said. "It's better after the first time."

She kissed the damp skin of his cheek. "I don't know how it could get any better."

He grinned down at her, flushed with male pride. "Nothing will ever separate us again," he vowed, gathering her into his protective embrace.

Chapter Twelve

Julie snapped out of her reverie as a boat went by on the river, whistle blowing and engines throbbing. She knew it would take Angel a while at the police station, and the last thing she wanted to do was to wait at her apartment, pacing anxiously and watching the hands of the clock crawl around until he arrived.

She was full of excitement and hope that she needed to tell someone. When she glanced at her watch she realized that Stef would be at work. Feeling like she would pop if she didn't do something, Julie thought of her mother and what her reaction might be if things *did* work out between Angel and Julie.

Walking back to the car, she decided that she had some groundwork to lay and some secrets to expose. No matter what was meant to happen between Angel and herself, she was proud of her feelings for him. Her parents might object, but she was no longer desperate for their approval. She had even married Brad for them.

There, it was finally out. She had married Brad because he was exactly the kind of son-in-law that her parents would like.

Julie slid behind the wheel and turned the key. She and Angel were destined to be together someday, if she had anything to say about it. She would die before she would allow her parents to hurt his feelings or his fierce pride, so now was as good a time as any to prepare them for the possibility that their grandchildren might have blood from two different heritages.

The thought of having Angel's children took Julie's breath away as she pictured chubby little boys with midnight-dark hair and little girls with brilliant blue eyes. When she pulled up in front of her parents' house, she was relieved to see her mother's Fiero parked in the driveway. Rushing up the steps, she opened the front door, took a deep, bracing breath and called out.

"Julianna! What are you doing here in the middle of the day? Not that you aren't always welcome, dear. Come in," her mother urged.

"I need to talk to you about something," Julie said before she could lose her nerve. "Are you busy?"

"Oh, this sounds serious. Come into the living room. Can I get you anything? Coffee? Tea?"

Julie shook her head. "No, thanks anyway. I can't stay too long." She wanted to get back to the apartment before Angel did. Julie stopped abruptly when she saw her father sitting on one of the couches wearing an old sweater and worn corduroy jeans. A box of tissues was next to him, and he held a mug of tea in both hands as if he needed the warmth. His nose was red, and his eyes had a dull sheen.

"Dad, are you all right?" He was rarely sick, and his lethargy alarmed Julie, who bent to give him a kiss.

He held her off with an upraised hand. "Better not," he said, turning his head away to cough. "I'll take a rain check."

"Your father has finally given in to his cold and decided to stay home and rest," her mother said, hovering over him until he shrugged off the hand she rested against his forehead. "He's probably already infected the rest of the company, going to work and sneezing all over everyone."

Julie had to smile at her father's sheepish expression as she sat down in a velvet tub chair at the end of the couch. He hated to miss a day's work, and usually went into the office no matter how he was feeling.

"I'm glad you're here, too," Julie told him as her mother perched on the opposite couch, looking expectant.

"There's something about the way you look," she said, studying Julie closely. "An inner glow. Has something happened?"

"I haven't been this excited in ten years," Julie said, smiling at the way her father's eyebrows rose. "Nothing's settled, and I'm probably jumping the gun, but I have to talk to you, to prepare you."

"That sounds ominous," her father said before surrendering to another fit of coughing.

"You've met someone," her mother guessed.

Suddenly Julie's courage failed her. Maybe she wasn't going about this right. What if she had totally misread Angel's feelings? She could be disappointing her parents needlessly, dragging up the past, revealing secrets about herself that would cause them pain because she had kept things from them at the time.

"Tell us, dear! You're driving us crazy!" Julie's mother was beginning to look exasperated at her silence.

"There are some things that you need to know," Julie said. "Things that happened a long time ago."

She thought she saw a shadow of premonition cross her mother's face. "Are you sure, dear? Sometimes it's better to leave the past where it belongs. Why would you need to bring it up now?"

Julie took a deep breath, remembering suddenly one of the reasons that she hadn't confided in her mother about Brad. There was a tinge of fear in her voice that didn't invite confidences. If the news was unpleasant, she preferred not to hear it. Undaunted this time, Julie pressed on.

"What I need to tell you is that I'm in love with Angel Maneros."

For a moment there was a stunned silence.

"The man who runs the center?" her mother asked. "The man I met at the charity benefit? Why, he's—" She glanced at Julie's father. "He's so well-known," she finished lamely. "You don't even know if he's going to stay around here."

"He's staying," Julie said confidently. "This is his home."

Her father cleared his throat, coughing again. "And how does Angel feel about you?" he asked hoarsely.

"I—I'm not sure, but I think he loves me, too."

"Well," her mother said, smoothing her hands over her skirt, "have the two of you made any plans?"

Julie felt as if she was picking her way through a thistle patch. What could she tell them? "Not yet. I'm meeting Angel at my apartment as soon as he's done at the jail—"

"Jail?" her parents echoed in unison.

Julie explained as briefly as possible about Angel's brother, assuring them both that Angel himself had nothing to do with the burglaries. She was grateful that they seemed to accept her explanation.

"I'm going to marry him if he asks me," she announced, clenching her hands together tightly in her lap.

"Are you sure, dear?" Her mother's brow was furrowed with concern. "You haven't known him all that long. Maybe you need more time to recover from your divorce."

Julie shook her head. "No, Mom. Our marriage was over a long time ago. I realize now that I only married him because of you."

"We never pressured you to marry him!"

Julie knew that her mother believed those words to be true.

"You always wanted me to belong," she said. "To have the right friends, the right clothes, to belong to the right sorority at college, to have the right major. I disappointed you over and over when I didn't fit in, when I wasn't popular, even when I majored in education."

Both her parents remained silent, their faces full of shock and hurt at her outburst.

Julie sighed and continued. This was getting more and more difficult. "I've known Angel a lot longer than you realize. We went to high school together."

"You wouldn't have been in the same circle of friends," her mother argued. "You did have friends in high school, despite what you say now."

"I knew the daughters of your friends. There's a difference." It was time to clear the air completely. "I had no circle of friends in high school," Julie said gently. "And for one whole year I only had Angel."

There was silence for a moment. "I don't understand," her father said. "Are you telling us that you dated him in high school? From what I read he lived in the worst part of town, didn't he? Wasn't his mother murdered in some drunken brawl?"

"She was killed accidentally at the tavern where she worked as a waitress, right before Angel went away. I was supposed to go away with him right after that, but I chickened out at the last minute and he left here alone."

"Oh, Julie." Her mother's voice was full of betrayal. "Why didn't you ever confide in us? How did you manage to see Angel then without us knowing anything about it? How did you even get to know him?"

"We managed. I'm sorry, Mom. I know this is a lot to lay on you now, but I want everything to be honest between us." Briefly she told them about the incident at the library, noticing how her father's face tightened when she mentioned her fear of the other boys. Then she touched lightly on hitting the dog, and how she and Angel became friends. Much of the rest of their relationship she omitted.

"I loved Angel then and I love him now," she said earnestly. "If he'll have me, I'm going to marry him and have his children." She took a deep breath, forcing the words out. "You wouldn't have accepted him in high school, you would have hated the idea of your daughter being with someone like him. Maybe you still hate it. I can't make you accept him now, but I hope you will. Either way, it's what I want."

She glanced at their faces before ducking her head and rising, her purse clutched tightly against her chest. She was shaking with the effort it had cost her to say what she had. She might never have their approval now, but suddenly it didn't seem important. Angel was all that mattered. Somehow over the past months she had become her own woman. Funny that she hadn't realized it until now.

"No matter how you might feel, I don't want you to hurt Angel," she said. "He has a lot of pride."

She was waiting for some kind of reply when both parents stood up, her mother crossing to take her father's hand.

"Darling, don't misunderstand," she said. "We only want your happiness. That's all we ever wanted, even when we were so happy that you chose Brad. How could we know..." Her voice faltered, then she went on. "After seeing what happened with a young man we approved of, how could you think we would object to someone you love now? I pray that he has the sense to love you as much as you obviously love him."

Julie's father nodded in agreement, his eyes suspiciously moist. "As you know, I've talked with Mr. Maneros more than once about his center and how our company can support it with corporate funding and job training. He's a fine young man, hard working and intelligent, and I have a lot of respect for what he's accomplished. I'm sure that I speak for both of us when I say that, if things work out the way you want, we will welcome Angel into the family with open arms."

Julie's eyes were full of tears when she reached out to embrace both parents. "Thank you," she mumbled as her father squeezed her hard, then pulled away to release a gigantic sneeze.

"Bless you," Julie said automatically.

"No, darling, bless you and your young man."

"We never realized how you felt," her mother said. "We wanted so much for you, but we always loved you.

No one could have wished for a better daughter. To learn now that you thought we disapproved of you, well, it hurts. I hope that you will believe me when I say we've always approved of you." Her eyes were brimming with sincerity and love.

Julie had to wipe at her own eyes. Now, when she had finally begun to understand that she had to live her own life and maké her own choices, the approval she had never thought she would win was shining on both her parents' faces. Tears ran down her mother's cheeks, and her father was busy blowing his nose.

"I love you both," she said. The clock in the hallway chimed the hour. "But now I have to go."

"We love you, too," her mother said. "Keep us posted?"

"Yes," her father said, following her to the door, coughing behind his hand. "Good luck. Bring Angel to see us soon."

"I hope to," Julie said, opening the front door. "Goodbye."

Starting the car, she wiped her cheeks with the back of her hand and wondered how different her life would have been if she had had enough faith to trust in her family before. There was no way to ever know, there was only the present and the future. Turning the corner, she headed back to the apartment, hoping that Angel would be there soon.

Angel tried not to reveal the emotions raging through him as he waited in an empty conference room for Luis to be brought to him. He had reviewed the charges with Detective Jenkins, who had congratulated him on his upcoming wedding. Hiding his confusion, he made a mental note to ask Julie about that when he saw her.

Then he concentrated on the detective's words, his despair increasing with every damning sentence.

"Hey, little bro, come down to bail me out?" Luis asked as the door of the conference room opened. A guard shut it behind Angel, who knew that the man would remain right outside.

"Why, Luis? Why did you do it?" he couldn't help but ask as his brother slumped into the chair across from him, tipping it onto its back legs as he eyed Angel with a confident grin. Confinement didn't seem to crush Luis's spirits in the least.

"Who says I did it?" he bluffed.

Angel slammed his open palm onto the table. "Don't con me!"

"Why not? That's what I am, in case you forgot, a con. Don't suppose you have any smokes on you?"

Angel shook his head, trying to keep a rein on his temper in the face of Luis's cocky attitude, the tone of his voice and the way he kept shifting away from Angel's stare.

"Did you bring my bail? I really want to get home and get out of these clothes," Luis said. He stopped when Angel shook his head.

"I didn't come to bail you out, Luis." His voice sounded dead, even to him.

Luis leaped up, knocking over his chair. "Didn't that damned judge set bail yet? Who do they think I am that they can keep me in here sitting on my butt? You got influence, why don't you use it? What good is your money and all your fame if your only relative is stuck in here?"

Something in Angel's face must have alerted him, and Luis stopped talking, sinking back into the chair.

"Angel? You're getting me out of here, aren't you?" His voice had a whiny edge to it now, his bravado drained away.

Angel hadn't realized it himself until he spoke the words aloud. "No, Luis. I'll pay for your lawyer, but after that you're on your own." Pain filled his chest, but he knew it was the right thing to do.

"Aw, come on, man. You don't mean that." Luis's voice rose sharply.

Angel stood up. "I'm afraid I do. I tried to help you, but I can't. You have to help yourself first, and you haven't wanted to do that."

"What kind of crap are you trying to hand me? You're my brother, my rich brother. Get me out of this dump."

Angel crossed to the door, sick at heart. When he turned back, Luis had swiveled around to face him, dark eyes blazing. "You're serious, aren't you? You never really cared about me, I was just another cause to you." His voice took on a wheedling tone. "What about all those times I stood up for you when you were little, when I took you places and bought you ice cream? Where's your gratitude, man?"

Angel winced, remembering all the other times Luis had brushed him off, had ignored him or "borrowed" money from Angel's piggy bank.

"Don't tell Mom or you'll be sorry," Luis would say.

Then he would grin and call Angel his best little bro and they would be buddies again. But somewhere along the way, battered by poverty and prejudice, Luis had changed. And, for a long time, Angel had refused to see it happening.

Luis came closer, but Angel brushed aside his grasping hand and looked him full in the face. "Why did you take my car for your dirty little jobs?" he asked softly.

Luis didn't answer, but the bitterness, the jealousy in his face spoke volumes.

"Goodbye, Luis," Angel said firmly. "You used me, just like you did when you took my allowance or made me lie to Mama for you, but this was the last time. You're still my brother. If you ever really sort things out, give me a call."

"Don't hold your breath," Luis snarled when he realized that Angel was serious about leaving him in jail.

There was nothing more to say. Angel opened the door and walked through it, his brother's shouted curses following him halfway down the hall.

Julie had just finished washing up and changing into a fresh blouse and shorts when she heard the Ferrari ease up to the curb outside. Taking a deep breath as she glanced in the mirror, she noticed the sparkle in her eyes and the way her cheeks glowed with color. For once she looked really pretty. Tucking a stray curl behind her ear, she went to open the front door.

There were lines on Angel's face that she hadn't noticed before, and his wide shoulders seemed to droop as he got out of the car. Obviously things at the jail had not gone well.

Looking up, Angel saw her waiting on the porch for him, and the smile that broke across his face made her catch her breath. He bounded up the steps and took her into his arms, holding her close as he buried his face in her hair.

"Just the sight of you standing here waiting for me is almost enough to wipe out the last hour," he said, voice muffled against her neck.

"Come inside. Was it very bad?"

His hand stayed possessively on her shoulder as he followed her in, shutting the door behind him. "It's over," he said. "I guess I didn't know Luis as well as I thought I did. All I can do for him now is to hire a good lawyer." He raised both hands in a gesture of defeat, then let them fall to his sides.

"I'm sorry." Julie glanced at the kitchen. "Do you want anything?"

"Just you." He sat down on the couch, pulling her beside him. "Did you call Connie?"

"Yes," Julie said. "I told her a little about Luis, and said that neither of us would be in today."

"Good girl." His response came out on a tired sigh, and he told her in clipped tones what had happened at the jail.

"I'm sorry," she repeated, stroking his cheek. "I hate to see you hurting like this. You tried so hard with him."

Angel tightened his arm across her shoulders. "Let's talk about happier things," he said, "like you and me."

She dipped her head, suddenly shy with him. "I'd like that."

"First of all," he continued, "let me say that I've come to realize at long last that you did the right thing in not leaving town with me before."

She opened her mouth to protest, but he laid a finger across her lips.

"The first years were rough. And I'm sure that, if you had been with me, I would never have taken the chances that made me so successful on the track."

"I'm so glad nothing happened to you," she burst out. "I couldn't bear it if you had been hurt."

His laugh was rueful. "I seem to have been charmed. When I think now of the risks I took..." He glanced at her face and changed the subject. "Anyway, you were right."

"Not entirely," she said. "I should have had faith in you. I should have really talked to you about it. Instead I tried to seduce you into staying in Clarkson."

His eyes narrowed. "Is that why you did it? I often wondered about your sudden change of heart. I should have been stronger, but I had wanted you for so long."

It was her turn to shush him. "I know, and I don't regret a thing. Except the last ten years." She blushed, realizing what she had revealed. "That wasn't the only reason why I gave myself to you. I loved you." She swallowed nervously. "I love you now," she said, watching his face.

He smiled tenderly, pulling her close and kissing her lips with a reverence that almost brought tears to her eyes. "I love you, too, babe. I never stopped. I just tried to ignore my feelings for a long time."

For a long moment he held her in his arms as she absorbed what he had told her. "I was always so proud of you," she said, still adjusting to the fact that he loved her. She ran one hand possessively up and down his arm. "I kept a scrapbook of clippings."

"Really? You didn't hate me for going alone?"

"I tried, but it was impossible. When Joey told me that you had left, I think I hated him."

"He told me you'd gotten married, but he didn't tell me about the divorce. I think he was trying to do me a favor, making sure I was really over you. Deep down I called myself a fool for coming back here, expecting you to be settled down with a family of your own." He thought for a moment. "What a shock to find out that you were divorced. I don't know if I would have been able to stay if you had still been married, with children."

Julie's fingers caressed his jaw. "I realized almost immediately that I had made a huge mistake. My parents had put on that elaborate wedding for us, and I was determined to make a go of it. When Brad began to—" her voice faltered but she made herself go on "—when he began to hit me, I thought it was my fault, because I couldn't love him."

Angel dropped a kiss on her forehead. "No, babe, it wasn't your fault. No one deserves to get beaten up like that." His hand curled into a fist. "When I think of what you went through, I feel so responsible. If only I had stayed—"

"Perhaps you were right to leave." She found herself more able to accept his side of things, more willing to see that what he had done was probably the only solution he could find at the time. "It would have been difficult for you here then."

"Are we arguing?" he asked lightly. "Both of us determined to hog the blame?"

Julie laughed, joy at his presence spilling out. "Let's agree to split it down the middle," she said. "After all, we were both so young."

"And now we're adults," he said. "And we know what we want."

She stared into his eyes, warmed by the flames she saw burning there. "Yes," she agreed.

Angel released her to slide off the couch.

"What are you doing?" she asked, alarmed, as he sank to one knee.

"What I've wanted to do for a very long time," he said softly, taking her hand in his. "Julie Remington, will you marry me? Will you live with me and bear my children, raise them with all the love we can give to them, and to each other, as long as we both live?" His voice quivered slightly at the end, and she realized how tense he was.

Julie's eyes filled with tears that spilled down her cheeks. "Oh, Angel, I love you so much," she said. "Yes, I want to marry you." She threw her arms around his neck and hugged him close, her heart pounding hard in her chest, her whole being flooded with joy.

When she pulled back to look at him, his eyes glimmered with moisture. "Thank you," he said, bending his head to place a kiss on the back of her hand. A lone tear dropped onto her skin, and tenderness flooded her heart. "I swear I'll do everything in my power to make you happy," he murmured. "If you lose your parents' approval because of me—"

Julie grabbed his shoulders excitedly. "No," she said. "That's not going to happen. I already told them."

His eyes widened, and he rose to sit back next to her on the couch. "What do you mean? What did you tell them?"

Julie glanced away, a little nervous at her earlier presumption. "I told them that I loved you," she said breathlessly. "That if you would have me, I was going to marry you."

Angel's shout of laughter startled her. "You're wonderful!" he exclaimed. "First you tell the whole police station about our night together, then you risk your parents' anger before I even get a chance to propose. After all the sneaking around before, I can't tell you how great it feels to finally have our love out in the open."

"I told them about before, too."

Abruptly he went still. "What did they say?"

"To bring you over to see them as soon as we had things settled."

His features softened with more love and contentment than Julie had ever dreamed she would see on his face again. "I think I'm going to get along with my in-laws very well," he said.

Angel lowered his head and covered Julie's mouth with what he meant to be a tender kiss. As soon as he felt her lips shape themselves to his, desire exploded within him. Dimly he remembered the first time he had kissed her after he came back. We'll never know what it's like to kiss when we no longer love, he thought. Our love will last forever.

His head was beginning to spin, his body was straining toward her, and his breath had backed up in his throat when he finally forced himself to set her gently aside.

"We have a lifetime for loving," he said, seeing the question in her eyes. "Right now I just want to savor the whole idea that we're finally, truly getting married. I've waited a long time for this moment."

"Do you think your mother would be pleased?" Julie asked, her gaze on his face.

Angel thought of his mother, how hard she had worked to give him a home. "I think my mother would be very pleased," he said.

"We'll be together at our center, too," Julie said. "Unless you're planning to fire me."

Angel searched her face to see if she was serious. "I like it when you say 'our' center," he said. "It wouldn't be nearly as great without you." He slid a strand of her hair through his fingers, tugging lightly. "When the babies come, we'll have a built-in day-care center right on the premises if you want to keep working. But of course if you decide to stay home, that will be okay, too." His smile deepened when he saw the adoration in her eyes. "Except that I'll miss you during the day. You'll have to promise to be there when I get home."

"Will we live in your house?" she asked. "I really love it, you know."

"I bought it with you in mind," he confessed. "I had pictured you there so many times that I was almost surprised to see Joey come out instead of you when I drove up."

A frown pinched her forehead. "About Joey," she said hesitantly. "I want you to know that he and I are getting along better, now. There won't be any problems with him living there."

Angel slapped a hand against his forehead. "I forgot to tell you. Joey wants to look into finding a new job. I expect he'll be moving in with Connie as soon as he does. I haven't told him yet, but the machining plant where he used to work is going to begin training apprentices soon. As a former employee, Joey will have first consideration."

"He's always been good with his hands," Julie remembered. "He used to enjoy working with cars."

"True. So after he moves out, it will be just the two of us." The thought of Julie sharing the house—and his bed—with him was enough to make a serious dent in Angel's self-control. "I think we should keep Consuela on as a part-time cleaning woman," he said, doing his best to ignore his growing passion. "If you're going to be at the center, we'll need her."

Julie nodded. "That's a good idea. It's a big house. Now, before we go tell my parents our news, would you like to see that scrapbook I kept all these years?" Before he could reply, she stood up.

Angel's fingers snared her wrist. "I'm very interested in the scrapbook and in talking to your parents," he said, rising to stand before her. "But first, there's something I can't wait to do any longer." He slipped the leash on his control and scooped Julie into his arms, cradling her slim body against his heart. "I need to possess you, *querida*," he said, looking into her eyes. "I've waited a lifetime for you, and I can't wait any longer. I want to be able to watch your face as I make you mine, and to tell you how much I love you when I'm exploding inside you."

As he carried her to the bedroom, Julie buried her face against his shoulder. "I love you, Angel," she murmured, heart so full of happiness she thought that she might burst. "I'll always love you."

He kicked the door shut behind them, and the last thing Julie saw before he lowered her to the bed was the poster of him watching them both. Before she transferred her attention to the real Angel, she blew his image a silent kiss.

*   *   *   *   *

Silhouette Special Edition

**MORE SPECIAL THAN EVER,
SAY THESE TOP AUTHORS:**

JO ANN ALGERMISSEN

"To me, writing—or reading—a Silhouette Special Edition *is* special. Longer, deeper, more emotionally involving than many romances, 'Specials' allow me to climb inside the hearts of my characters. I personally struggle with each of their problems, sympathize with the heroine, and almost fall in love with the hero myself! What I truly enjoy is knowing that the commitment between the hero and heroine will be as lasting as my own marriage—forever. That's special."

TRACY SINCLAIR

"I hope everyone enjoys reading Silhouette Special Editions as much as I enjoy writing them. The world of romance is a magic place where dreams come true. I love to travel to glamorous locales with my characters and share in the excitement that fills their lives. These people become real to me. I laugh and cry with them; I rejoice in their ultimate happiness. I am also reluctant to see the adventure end because I am having such a good time. That's what makes these books so special to me—and, I hope, to you."

SSE-A2

1989
IS THE YEAR
OF THE MAN!

What makes a romance? A special man, of course, and Silhouette Desire celebrates that fact with *twelve* of them! From Mr. January to Mr. December, every month has a tribute to the Silhouette Desire hero—our **MAN OF THE MONTH!**

Sexy, macho, charming, irritating... irresistible! Nothing can stop these men from sweeping you away. Created by some of your favorite authors, each man is custom-made for pleasure—*reading* pleasure—so don't miss a single one.

Mr. January is Blake Donavan in RELUCTANT FATHER by Diana Palmer
Mr. February is Hank Branson in THE GENTLEMAN INSISTS by Joan Hohl
Mr. March is Carson Tanner in NIGHT OF THE HUNTER by Jennifer Greene
Mr. April is Slater McCall in A DANGEROUS KIND OF MAN by Naomi Horton
Mr. May is Luke Harmon in VENGEANCE IS MINE by Lucy Gordon
Mr. June is Quinn McNamara in IRRESISTIBLE by Annette Broadrick

And that's only the half of it—
so get out there and find your man!

Silhouette Desire's
MAN OF THE MONTH...

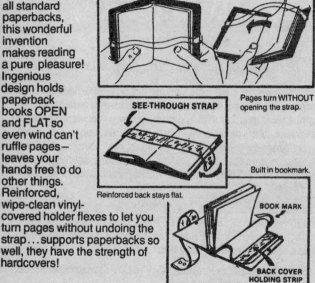

COMING IN APRIL

NAVY BLUES
Debbie Macomber

Between the devil and the deep blue sea . . .

At Christmastime, Lieutenant Commander Steve Kyle finds his heart anchored by the past, so he vows to give his ex-wife wide berth. But Carol Kyle is quaffing milk and knitting tiny pastel blankets with a vengeance. She's determined to have a baby, and only one man will do as father-to-be—the only man she's ever loved . . . her own bullheaded ex-husband! Can the wall of bitterness protecting Steve's battered heart possibly withstand the hurricane force of his Navy wife's will?

You met Steve and Carol in NAVY WIFE (Special Edition #494)—you'll cheer for them in NAVY BLUES (Special Edition #518). (And as a bonus for NAVY WIFE fans, newlyweds Rush and Lindy Callaghan reveal a surprise of their own....)

Each book stands alone—together they're Debbie Macomber's most delightful duo to date! Don't miss

NAVY BLUES
Available in April,
only in *Silhouette Special Edition*.
Having the "blues" was never
so much fun!

SE518-1